Darkness Before Mourning, Volume I

The Announcers

For Angela & Ted
It took quite awhile
for its arrival, but it's
finally here.
All the best

Gary Parker
8/31/15

Darkness Before Mourning, Volume I

The Announcers

by

J. G. Perkins

[signature: Greg Perkins]

Chatwin Books
Seattle 2015

Darkness Before Mourning,
Volume I: ***The Announcers***

Edited by Phil Bevis and Geoff Wallace,
with the assistance of Amanda Knox.

Series cover design, and cover design for this volume by
Stephanie Podmore. Rear cover photograph of the author
© Annie Brulé, 2014. Interior design by Phil Bevis.

This is a work of fiction. No resemblance is intended to
any living person.

Copyright © J. G. Perkins, 2015
Editorial & design copyright © CHATWIN LLC, 2015

All rights reserved.

ISBN-10: 1633980022
ISBN-13: 978-1633980020

Chatwin Books
www.chatwinbooks.com

Dedicated to my father

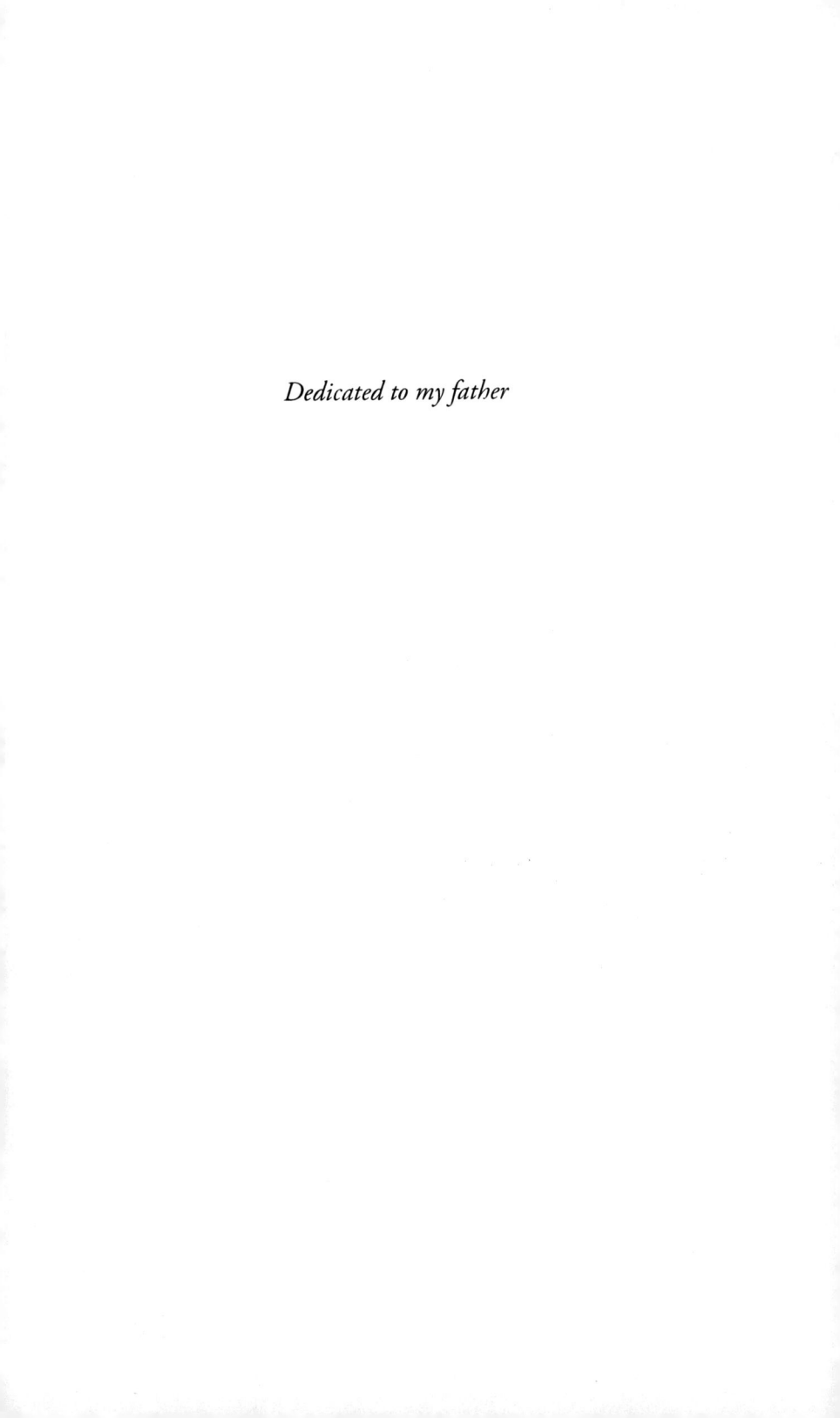

Contents

Introduction: *As I Remember It*   *p.11*

The Announcers, Chapter 1   *p.15*

Publisher's Afterword   *p.220*

"The past is never dead. It's not even past."

William Faulkner, *Requiem for a Nun*

Introduction

As I Remember It

I came of age in the Midwest of the 1950s. If you were there, I'd like to think you understand what that means. Over the years, as the focus of America's culture and economy shifted toward the coasts, the Midwest became the subject of jokes, a flyover country full of rusty factories, failing communities, and outdated morality. But in the 1950s, the Midwest mattered—it was the heart of the nation.

America in 1955 believed itself a nation of shared faith. Faith in the American way. Faith in God, faith in family, faith in prosperity created by hard work. Faith in a better future for the next generation. Faith in its righteousness after victory in two world wars, followed by a crusade to defend free peoples from Communism. Faith in baseball.

America's faith in itself was bolstered by economic prosperity. Thriving industries, high employment, high rates of homeownership, a boom in sales of consumer goods like autos and major appliances, expansion of higher education making college a reality for many families for the first time, a boom in science and technical innovation—all largely concentrated in the geographical and cultural heartland—the Midwest.

Flashes of memory—Plain-speaking people. People giving a helping hand to strangers stopped on the side of the road. Covered bridges. Hay rides. Cherry Coke and hamburgers. As far as the eye could see—corn and wheat readied for harvest in rectangular fields. Oven-like heat seizing your breath. The sharp smell of ice crystals glistening in the air. Torrents of blinding, soaking rain.

J. G. Perkins

Teeth-jarring thunderclaps and the sun re-emerging above endless fields of flowers. Baseball on a summer afternoon—the jolt of the bat in your hands, players chattering in the field, my dad's voice from the announcer's booth.

The Midwest was the embodiment of America's common faith—towns and cities filled with thrifty, hard-working people who all looked like each other and bought into a common set of beliefs. If you looked or were seen as different, you were apart. Television's *Father Knows Best* might as well have been set in Kokomo, Indiana—where I grew up. Our town thrived—there were good jobs for anyone who wanted one. And churches—churches everywhere. It seemed like every city block had at least one.

Religious faith went beyond the church steps. Expressions of it were everywhere—in my public school classrooms and their weekly Bible lessons, on television, radio, and in newspapers. It was assumed that everyone believed in God. Faith was the glue that held Kokomo together.

All you had to do was believe, and life had purpose and meaning. All you had to do was believe, and St. Peter would be waiting at the Pearly Gates. All you had to do was believe, and everlasting life was the automatic result. All you had to do was believe.

My family had a problem with that. America, faith, and the Midwest were thriving, and my family—Mom, Dad, my sister, and I—should have been thriving along with it. Instead, we were about to experience our own unique prelude to the Midwest's decline.

For those who shared it, the American Dream was wonder-

The Announcers

ful. I awakened from part of that dream early and watched, in one way or another, much of the rest of the country follow over several decades. Some are still asleep. Like many of the awakened, I found that my dream had elements of a nightmare. And while I treasure truth above all else, I envy those who are still dreaming.

Chapter 1

As usual, it took death to bring me back to Kokomo. In the thirty-eight years since my father died in 1958, this had been the general rule. Returning home in a helter-skelter fashion was the last thing I expected to be doing—until that phone call at 5:30 a.m. A call at that hour is never good news, and this wasn't an exception. *There's no one left to die,* I thought as I hurried to answer—I was wrong.

Uncle Mike was dead. "A sudden heart attack last night," my cousin said, sounding as calm as if he were reading soybean futures in a farm report. Uncle Mike was dead, consigned to nothingness like all the rest. He'd been the last of my mother's brothers, and the last of my family in Kokomo. I hadn't heard from my uncle in years and hadn't missed him—or Kokomo, either.

This is how I wound up in a rented '96 Ford Taurus driving on a road back to a place I didn't want to revisit.

My experience with death went way back, and even though this was someone I wasn't interested in having in my life, his absence still hit me like a blow to the face. Although I didn't have time for Mike while he was alive, surprisingly the pain of losing him was as sharp as that from past deaths of those I was close to. The Taurus's plastic steering wheel stayed obedient within my clenched hands, and my eyes stayed on the road, but my mind was someplace else—a movie theater from long ago.

I was thirteen. Mom sent me to the movies to get me out of the way. Somehow I knew my grandmother had come to find me—and I knew why before I saw her, so I turned around in my seat. When I finally caught a glimpse of her, she was walking down the aisle, looking for me. I wanted to hide but couldn't. I knew that she was going to tell me my dad was dead. And I knew I'd never have a chance to say goodbye to him. And—

Squeezing the wheel even harder, I wished I'd weaseled out of attending Mike's funeral. I'd had to scramble to make last-minute travel arrangements to fly to the small Midwestern town I'd fled long ago, and I was having trouble thinking of why. After hurried packing, a cramped flight, and a slew of inconveniences, I finally approached my hometown, my mind churning like a maelstrom—the weather was clear today, but I was caught in a storm forty years in the past.

Dad was always sick, or at least it seemed that way to me—even up to the time his life came to a screeching halt on that Thursday afternoon as I sat in the movie theatre, watching some forgotten science fiction thriller, subconsciously waiting for news that I somehow already knew.

It was strange that I knew what was happening because I'd never been told my dad was dying. He was sick, and clearly I knew something was happening, but so many things were simply not spoken of in Midwestern America in the 1950s. What did I admit to myself—and what did I hide from myself? I've always had that uncertainty—ever since my father didn't come home from the hospital and I finally realized he never would.

The familiar sight of the four hundred-foot-tall gas tank on Route 31, sitting like a sentinel at the edge of Kokomo, makes me realize I'm going the wrong way. My hands intended to steer the car to Mike's viewing, but instead the car drove as if on autopilot, programmed for only one possible destination: the Northside Little League baseball field. Northside Little League—the thought brings with it images of Dad announcing from the scorekeeper's booth above the field while I played right field for the Nationals.

But first I have to stop at the intersection with Alto Road. If the Taurus turned east, it would eventually get to the graveyard where Dad's buried. My ashes will be buried alongside him one day. I look in the direction of the cemetery, but the car drives on.

The Taurus is taking me on a road I could never drive by myself. It's unlikely Northside will still be there after so many years, but I've avoided it like the plague ever since the nightmares started. *Dad was never there when I was looking for him.* How old was I when I began having those dreams? Seventeen. Eighteen at the latest.

Before the dreams, I used to ride my bike and later drive my car out to Northside, looking desperately for signs. Signs that my father had ever been there.

As I pass the American Legion on Mulberry, I see the town has fallen on hard times. Really hard times, with dilapidated houses and trash in the yards. I make sure the doors are locked—not quite the homecoming I was looking for.

Then it hits me: I thought I'd come back for my uncle, but I'm really here for my dad. Even though I've been back to Kokomo a couple dozen times in the last four decades, it's as though the gap of all those intervening years has vanished in the blink of an eye, and all that's left is an adolescent boy in a thriving town looking across time at a weathered man in a down-at-heels city. And I sense the presence of my dad in a way that I haven't since his death. Not even the nightmares compare to how real this feels. The nightmares had made me afraid to think of my father... but it's different now.

And while I'm thinking about it, Northside's baseball diamond is the single most important source for my memories of my dad, and the diamond's getting closer and closer. With each turn and the passage of each familiar street, I can hear echoes of chatter from baseball games decades past growing louder: "New guy at the plate... easy out... piece of cake... easy out... Hey batter... hey batter batter SWING!"

Chatter in baseball is meant to distract the batter, and everyone on the field is expected to contribute. From his vantage point in the scorekeeper's box, Dad would always make a special point of reminding me of that whenever he couldn't hear me loud and clear from my spot in right field.

"Shout it out if you have to!" he instructed me. "You've got to be heard." Sometimes I got hoarse trying to live up to his expectations. Although I couldn't see him up there behind the backstop, I always sensed his presence. And when I wasn't playing I sat by his side. He taught me how to keep score—for much more than baseball.

I'm suddenly realizing that the chatter... and these voices... aren't memories—I'm actually hearing them around me now, like some kind of auditory hallucination. But I'm not that kind of guy. I'm a scientist and the most rational person I know. The kind of guy you could call Jack—like me. John Lewis if you're feeling formal. If I can't touch it, feel it, or prove it in a lab, I don't believe it. Hearing voices—baseball chatter, imaginary voices, or otherwise—should be bothering me more. As I get closer to the field, the chatter's getting louder. But it's not a distraction. Somehow, it's why I'm here.

"Steeeerike one! Nuthin' but air."

I'm turning left onto North Street. Finally, I come to an intersection that looks exactly the same as when I grew up. It's here in front of me after all these years, with its hardware store on one corner, and I can't tell the slightest difference between the store then and now.

Or perhaps I just want it to be that way, and if I looked closer it would be dilapidated like everything else—myself included. And now I'm in the driver's seat rather than the passenger's—an important distinction, and one that's different from the silence that's permeating the car now just like it did during the fifty or so times Dad and I rode to Northside together for games.

Fifty... it seems like nothing. Were our trips to the field so few? We rarely talked during any of our rides, and never about anything important. I guess I was the one waiting for him to start talking, and when he didn't, I just let the silence win.

Sad, particularly since so much needed to be said. Like how glad I was to have him back home after that dreadful December when he was away at Mayo Clinic and I didn't know when he'd be coming back. Like how much I loved him. So much needed to be said or asked. Like the reason for his operation. And why he was so skinny and yellow.

My fingers are strangling the goddamn steering wheel.

"Steeeerike two! Didn't even see it."

The baseball chatter is really loud now. It sounds exactly like it did when I was a kid standing out in right field, screaming as loud as anyone. I should be getting really close to the park, but now nothing seems familiar to me. The houses and trees look strange—so different from when I was younger, when it seemed like they never changed. Now, it seems as though things never stay the same. And somehow, it feels like it all should be the same as it was during those two summers with my dad.

I was always chomping at the bit, so eager to get to the ballpark and get on the field with my major league cleats—too eager to comprehend what was happening to Dad, let alone notice him struggling behind the steering wheel of our '56 Ford. Nor did I understand the score on those summer afternoons, or even which game we were playing.

My father was dying—dying while engaged in a Herculean effort to hold himself together for my benefit, a desperate pretense that everything was fine. And the less that was said, the easier the pretense.

"Keep your eye on the ball no matter what," he might have said.

"Always watch where the catcher wants the ball to be thrown."

Might have said—

Because I don't remember him uttering those words.

Because it was the things he didn't say that I needed the most.

Anyway, it's the images and not the words that I remember—or even how his voice sounded. And so many of the images I have in memory are images that I don't want.

The yellow from jaundice.

The colostomy bag.

Blood.

And so much else—

The signs were all there. He would die in less than a year after the last of those two seasons. How did I miss them? Who am I trying to kid? Only myself.

The image of the ballpark is so very clear. What am I about to find there now…? I lost count long ago of all the times I've returned there in my mind—returned to that elevated scorekeeper's box just behind and above home plate, where two chairs and a table overlooked the field. We sat there together behind a microphone feeding into a loudspeaker system. A protective backstop shielded us from foul tips, but we still jumped every time they hit the fence.

Surrounding the ballpark was a wire fence with neatly capped white wooden posts that always seemed to be freshly painted. A bright white paint that was never soiled—not even where my head collided with the fence during tryouts. The outfield seemed so big, so expansive. Stands flanked the first- and third-base sides of the infield; my mother and sister sat on the third-base side during games.

Oaks towered in the front yards of the houses across from the ballpark. I've never seen trees this green, and neither the houses nor the trees ever seemed to change. Looming in the background was The Globe American Company, a large white brick building. All I knew was that stoves were made inside, and you could see kids playing on its loading dock.

After our two seasons together ended, Dad took my cap, my award plaques and his own announcer's plaque, nailed them to a finished wooden board and hung it on my bedroom wall. I admired seeing my plaques next to dad's—it was almost as though we'd played side by side on the same team. Almost...

Shortly after this, our family was walking toward Highland Park Stadium to see the Dodgers, Kokomo's minor league baseball team, for Little League recognition night when I heard a man calling out my name from behind. After he repeated my name two or three times, I turned and identified myself.

"You're a lucky boy," the man said. "You've been selected to be batboy for this evening's game."

I was lucky indeed. During the course of the evening, I met Pete Reiser, who managed the Dodgers and would have been in the Hall of Fame if he'd learned how to avoid crashing into the outfield wall. I also met Tommy Davis and Orlando Cepeda, who gave me their cracked bats as souvenirs.

There's chatter at every game—including this one.

"Steeeerike three! You're out!"

"Look at this boy," Cepeda said to his teammates. "He's good-looking enough to be in the movies."

Lucky indeed—

I enjoyed the experience, completely unaware of why I was

chosen. Dad never told me. It took me until I was nearly thirty before I figured it all out. I was the only player in the league whose dad was dying of cancer.

While keeping the secret, Kokomo was being as kind to me as it could possibly be.

My dad made it to thirty-nine. Before he died, he taught me how to keep score—in baseball, and in life. Either way you count it, not even making it to forty—it's just not a regulation game.

Chapter 2

My side trip to Northside isn't proving to be as easy as I thought it was going to be. Not by a long shot. All of this crap with my father should have been sorted out decades ago.

I'm close to the baseball field, and the chatter's strangely stopped, but now there's a familiar smell in the air—a smell that shouldn't exist, something that just can't be. It's the smell of Dad's pipe—like the cheap aromatic blend he used to smoke. I haven't encountered it since his death. And don't think for a moment that I haven't searched wherever I've gone.

Smoking was the one private thing my dad could do at home without interruption, and not even cancer could take away my dad's enjoyment of his pipe.

It *can't* be Dad's. Maybe my mind's playing tricks on me. It can only be coming from Mulberry Street behind me. Geographically. Chronologically. I don't know which is farther now: a few blocks, or the 1950s.

More specifically, even if it were still the 1950s, the aroma could only be wafting in from one place—the living room in the little white house on Mulberry Street—because that's the only place Dad smoked back then. We lived in that house from the time I was four or five years old until the time he died. Eight or nine years seemed like a minor eternity back then—the majority of my childhood—but seem like a short span now. He'd only smoke sitting in his favorite chair. One time he threw a match in the waste basket and set it on fire. Mom yelled at him, but I can only hear her voice and not his. No matter how hard I try, that's the way it is—I can never hear his voice even when I know what he said.

Sometimes I don't even remember what he said, but I remember what he did. No voice, only I see his face peering at me in surprise. I might have been three or four years old. Mom, my sister Ann, and I were in the kitchen. Mom was standing directly in front of me, her back turned as she prepared supper. Ann was across the room in her crib, and I was standing on the heater. I reached up to grab a frayed wire and my body was instantly paralyzed by electrical current. I couldn't speak or move, but Ann was wailing, and I would've been electrocuted if Dad hadn't heard the commotion and rushed into the room to rescue me.

Another image flashes—I'm standing in front of the house and watching for Dad to come home from his job at the post office. I'm straining my eyes to catch sight of him—a small, unmistakable shape off in the distance, gradually growing larger—and when I can finally make out his features, a thrill surges through me. But why would I have such a feeling this time? Are all kids so excited to see their dads come home? Or is this tied in with him dying so young?

If remember correctly, Dad was happy to see me too.

Dad and I, his arm around me, stand in front of Kokomo's Memorial Gymnasium. The gym was in the final stages of completion and for a while would be the largest in the country. Later, during the basketball season of '57–'58—the last one prior to his death—I can see Dad sitting across the court from me, chewing gum. We both were in the front row—but why was Dad sitting across from me? I'm racking my brain for answers, but every reason I grasp dissolves like smoke between my fingers.

The Announcers

Although I have a near-photographic memory, my adolescent years in Kokomo feature remotely few images and memories. Most of the memories I do have are dominated by fear, pain and loss. But for the most part, those years seem largely shrouded in a fog of forgetful numbness.

Perhaps that's why this series of powerful, flashing images forces me to pull over to the curb. There. A second will be all I'll need to collect my thoughts before heading to Northside. This latest excursion down memory lane is throwing me off balance. For a moment, I wonder if there really is pipe smoke drifting over from Mulberry Street, but of course that can't be. I never meant to go back there, since the neighborhood's really run down compared to how it was when we lived there. Our house was barely recognizable the last time I was there—it was falling apart and seemed a lot smaller than I remembered. Most of the trees in the yard were gone except the one Dad planted in the back, which was huge. I remember feeling relieved that at least something from those years was thriving.

Like the work that Dad put into maintaining the yard, he went to great lengths in everything that he did. His smoking station was the classic example. It wouldn't really be worth mentioning if not for how much that spot clearly mattered to him—and that it was the first thing you saw when you walked in the front door. Nothing fancy—recliner, footstool, and smoking stand. Once in a while, when he wasn't home, I would sit in his recliner, once with my fifth-grade girlfriend. Both of us fit in it with room to spare.

Dad usually went straight to his recliner after getting home from one of his jobs. He spent most of his time working at the post office, and he had a second job making tire weights on weekends. He'd come through the back door, walk up a few steps, and take a sharp left turn at the refrigerator. Then it was through the kitchen and dining room and into his chair.

Even then I wasn't too young to pick up on things—he was dog-tired and dragging his feet. Sometimes I wondered how he even made it to his chair, but he did. I knew enough not to bother him until he got settled in and lit his pipe. Mom had made things as easy for him as she possibly could. His matches, ashtray, tobacco, and pipe were always neatly arranged on the smoking stand next to the chair, so Dad could fire up his pipe as quickly as possible.

As memory replays this, I could almost forget how sick Dad was. Though as I realize now, his movements were very deliberate, as if moving in slow motion. With what I know today, I'm surprised he could move at all.

Dad would close his eyes and take a big sniff of his pipe tobacco in its pouch before doing anything else. At that one moment, the expression on his face was different than any other time I remember from those years. Serene. Satisfied. Contented. Despite the fact that he was dying, the aroma of his tobacco seemed to free his mind from everything else.

One day before he got home from work, I took a big whiff of his tobacco. Cheap as it was, I can't imagine any tobacco smelling better—a slight fragrance of cherry wood. Years after he died, I realized that I'd always chosen cherry wood for the built-in shelves in my home libraries.

After he was gone, Mom told me something I've always wanted to forget, but never could. Dad bought his first pouch of this tobacco the week before the first blood stains appeared on the rear of his shorts. The appearance of that special tobacco smell overlaps with my dad changing from youth—healthy and strong—to what I now know was a dying man. My last memory of what feels like my real Dad is of him sitting on the footstool, his head in his hands. Then he went to the hospital and died.

Mom and Dad ignored the first stains until several months had passed—Mom finally made such a ruckus that, if Dad wanted peace at home, he had to see a doctor. First came the Kokomo doctor—a general practitioner who was the best the town had to offer—who found something very suspicious.

"Not quite right" was the phrase used in 1950s Kokomo to describe this sort of thing. In actuality, it was a large tumor, growing more lethal with each passing minute. At this relatively early stage, immediate removal of the suspicious something was of the essence if Dad was to have any chance.

From Kokomo's medical minor leagues, he was sent to a big league doctor in Indianapolis, which was where, as Mom put it, people who were "really sick" had to go. This told me that Dad was really sick, even if I didn't comprehend what that meant. Even worse, the tumor was considered well beyond Indianapolis's medical skills. This left only Mayo Clinic as a last resort, but even their all-star team of doctors could only give him a short reprieve.

The aroma from Dad's pipe is really strong now. Rolling down the window doesn't make the slightest amount of difference but, feeling short of breath, I keep it down.

Sometimes, as I sat on the footstool, I'd see Dad lighting up, savoring the first few puffs. In my memory, he'd often glance at me—three or four hurried glances with eyes that were truly awful, drowning in pain and exhaustion. In my imagination, this is a foretelling of leaving behind a young and attractive widow, his daughter, and his son, the Little Leaguer, and their shared love of baseball.

Sometimes after Dad's initial three or four draws on his pipe he'd close his eyes just like he did in church. Several times—I don't remember how many—I got brave and asked him if he was tired. "I'm just resting my eyes," he said. "Just resting my eyes," he repeated, his voice suddenly loud and—

His voice. I'm actually hearing his voice! This feels like a breakthrough.

As soon as Dad told me this he turned his head away from me. Back then I thought this was peculiar, but not so now. Screw loose or not I've FINALLY heard Dad speak twice, the second time louder than the first. It's the first time since I arrived in Kokomo, although I've been listening since I entered the city limits. I've finally heard him speak loud and clear from Mulberry Street and forty years away. If I close my eyes, he could be sitting next to me in the front seat of the Taurus—

But my eyes are open, so I know Dad's not here. I'd believe I was totally rational, but I'm still smelling his pipe smoke.

Chapter 3

"I'm resting my eyes." Dad's voice is coming through loud and clear again—with me still sitting by the curb not going anywhere for the time being, the aroma of his pipe smoke still as strong as ever. I can't stay parked here much longer or the cops will stop and check me out. An out-of-state license plate doesn't help either. The locals are extremely leery of strangers, and I guess I qualify as one since I know hardly anyone here anymore. It probably would've been better if it'd been that way when I lived here, too.

But before I can pull away from the curb, my mom's voice shows up, and for a second, I'm puzzled. A moment passes as her words seem to make the aroma of pipe smoke vanish, and then I realize that she's talking about something my father never told me about. Her voice weaves together slim details and sentences gleaned from conversations over many years, forming the tapestry of a narrative as she describes the day she and my dad were waiting at Mayo Clinic for the results of his surgery. After what seemed like countless hours sitting in the cold sterile room, where the only visual relief was the pattern in the linoleum floor, a young doctor in a crisp white lab coat, clipboard in hand, clearly uncomfortable, walked into the room. His final pronouncement changed everything.

That was when my parents decided to lie to my sister and me. They lied from that first minute to his dying day, and the whole town of Kokomo lied with them. The truth only came years later—in dribbles—and was never complete.

I've imagined the truth of that moment in Mayo Clinic so

many times over the years, and it plays in my head like a scene from an old movie—and it's playing right now, unwelcome as always. The young doctor, fidgeting with the charts on his clipboard, is stalling. My parents know it, and they're impatient for the truth.

"I can see right off the bat you're a little more energetic today. The transfusions we've been giving you appear to have given you a boost. They're real energizers—like shots in the arm." The doctor speaks to my dad, ignoring my mom. "No doubt about it—the red blood cell count is definitely up—and you wouldn't have any gas in your fuel tank without that going for you."

My dad slumps and his voice grows weaker. "I'll have to take your word for it, doctor. I can't say that I'm feeling any different than I did yesterday or the day before."

My mom glares at my dad and coughs. "I can tell a difference if you can't!" she snaps. "Didn't I mention that to you just before the doctor arrived? You're noticeably stronger."

My dad just shakes his head, forcing the doctor to reemphasize his point. "That makes two of us, then—and the majority rules." Shifting to my mom, he says, "Not to change the subject, but I see that you haven't totally shaken your bug."

"Not totally," my mom says, taken aback and irritated by anyone mentioning her illness. "But... but I'm just about—"

The doctor interrupts her. "For a while, we thought we were going to have to admit you as well. You were as close to pneumonia as you can get without having it, and I'm not totally sure you *didn't* have it. But we have much better drugs these days—like antibiotics—and I'm happy to say they give us a chance to work miracles like never before." He looks at the clipboard again. "I'm happy to say all that's behind us now," the doctor says. "Now, as I was saying about our patient here—"

My parents both try and interrupt to get an answer about the operation, but the doctor rifles through his charts again, delaying the inevitable for a while longer. "Red blood cell count is much better. With the red blood cells behaving so well, there's only one more little detail to take care of before we can send you off back home. You..." The doctor hesitates. "You've—how can I say this delicately... you've got... you've got to be able to pee on your own. Your bladder's in shock as a result of the operation. I see this all the time. Bladders are finicky that way. Always have been; always will be. After the operation you just had it takes a while for your bladder to return to its old—"

My parents' impatience is palpable. They're glaring at the doctor.

More flipping of charts. "Given the amount of time we had to work on him, Tom pulled through the procedure quite well—far better than I or anyone else expected. But as you both know, there was a lot that needed to be done surgically. You came to us... very late. It was much more than we here at Mayo's usually have to contend with. I'm referring to your operation. We had to take out as much as I've ever seen—if not more."

Finally, anxiety triumphs over manners and my parents both shout: "TELL US!"

"It was impossible for us to remove all of the cancer we

found." He mentions lymph node involvement, metastases, the liver, turning yellow. "You have a year, probably two, three years—maximum."

The doctor exits the room, his words—his announcement—echoing like a death sentence in a silent courtroom. The echoes continued on the long train ride home. The lies started with the verdict, and are still resonating.

Desperation—the great deceiver.

Chapter 4

I'm still sitting in the car on North Street; I haven't stopped remembering. The flashes of memory are coming in faster—racing through my brain like they don't want to stay long—and it's the letters coming to me now: the letters written to my sister and me from Mayo Clinic in Rochester, Minnesota. It was a first for our parents—they did it to make up for their physical absence. Neither ever said as much, though. They didn't have to.

Mom started writing us right after Thanksgiving and ended the day after Christmas; Dad wrote only one brief note on the eve of his surgery. They were very positive and loving letters, written to bolster our spirits. How well they pulled this off has amazed me more and more with each passing year—

Ann and I were sitting at the kitchen table. Three stacks of letters, in front of us: two with letters addressed to us singly, and a third addressed to both of us. Each stack was held together by rubber bands and represented everything we felt was wrong, wrapped in neat bundles. We were still trying to continue as we had before Mom and Dad left, drawing on the bundles as if they were fuel.

This was the first time Mom and Dad had ever left us. Ann and I sat in our usual places, as if our parents were about to join us. Their empty chairs at the table seemed to make it harder to talk. As the silence became awkward, I held up my stack of letters. "Dad's written only once," I said bluntly, "and that was two days before his operation."

My voice startled Ann. After a moment, she held up her

own stack of letters. "I know," she said. "All of these are from Mom."

"It seems like they've been gone forever," I said. "Remember what they told us. Dad had to have an operation." This simple response did not convince Ann.

"Why?" Ann asked. "Is he really sick?" Dad's illness was still not firmly established in Ann's reality; its brushstrokes were too wide for a third grader's mind.

I suddenly coughed and wheezed, trying to hide my confusion from Ann. Yes, I thought, *definitely sick. But sick with what?* "I think so. He must be. If he wasn't really sick they wouldn't be keeping him there for so long." I coughed and wheezed more loudly than before.

"Hey, are you getting sick again?" Ann said, her voice rising in alarm. "You've been coughing and throwing up ever since they left."

My fit subsided, and I eyed Mom's letter of the day. It was addressed to "My two sweet lug heads"—an odd and unusual tone. Re-reading this letter over the years, and given what she'd just experienced, I've always marveled that she could write to us at all.

But she did, in a letter full of lies. Lies of commission mixed with lies of omission. She joked about the weather—fifteen below with the temperature falling. That's what it was in Minnesota. "A cheap imitation of the Antarctic, but not that far off."

Next in Mom's letter was my cough and throwing up. My asthma, in other words. I never should have brought it up, but

I had in a previous letter. I downplayed it as a single episode and that was all. Two at most. I never told her that my asthma—the coughing and wheezing—had occurred at least once every day since they left. And that I'd thrown up in every room in the house. Lying was clearly a family talent.

I missed them too much to weigh them down with worries about me. I was afraid they were never coming back. In some respects they never did.

Mom provided a preview of how Dad looked toward the end of her letter: *Now darlings, I'd better explain something. Daddy isn't fat yet (I don't want him too fat) so don't expect too much when we get home. He looks about the same as he did when he left.*

I tried to remember how Dad appeared as they were leaving on the train. That gray, gloomy day—the day after Thanksgiving—my world was out of kilter in so many ways that little really registered with me. The way Dad looked wasn't one of those things I noticed or remembered.

What I do remember was Dad patting me on the head and telling me to be a good boy—

Mom crying—

Being so confused and sad—

The two of them waving from the window at us as they got smaller and smaller and smaller.

While our parents were gone, our mother's parents and brother, Norman, stayed with us. This made the time Mom and Dad were away as bearable as it could possibly be. Our grandparents didn't make much of an impression, but Uncle Norman was fun, chasing us around the house singing "This

Old Man." He played endless games with us and bought us several rounds of Christmas presents. He really tried.

Ann and I had really high expectations about our parents returning home. Mom said Dad would be sent home from the hospital when his bladder recovered and he could pee. Something about this came across as funny to us—we still hoped that this could happen in time for Christmas.

Ann was becoming uncomfortable with my coughing attacks and tried to divert my attention. "W-w-what do you want for Christmas?" she asked.

"F-for everything t-to be as it was."

"You mean it might not be?" Ann said, surprised at the possibility for the first time.

"I don't know," I said, another cough erupting like a small volcano. "Mom did write that they'd be here if they possibly could."

Ann stomped her foot. "They have to be!"

"And we'll have everything ready to m-make it easier for them when they get here," I reassured her.

After all, dears, Mom wrote, *he's had quite an operation, which I'll explain to you both when I can talk to you.* Except Mom could *never* talk to us to really explain the details of Dad's operation. The appearance of a colostomy bag on Dad's side should have told us a great deal—but somehow it never did, even though it was always full of shit and blood. Cancer was never mentioned. It was a word that people in Kokomo avoided like the plague.

The Announcers

I just didn't want you to think that he changed a lot—that will come a little later. I'm so glad he's eating so much—every bite means more strength.

There's a picture of Dad and me shortly after he finally returned. We're standing side by side, and I was every bit as skinny as him. Thin as a rail—maybe thinner. Dad would never be fat again, or ever really look healthy.

"Never" is the key word here. I would've seen that glimmer of health if it ever came, because I never stopped looking. The first instant I saw him, Mom had to help him get off the train so he wouldn't fall to the ground. And when I came over to him for a hug, I could feel him leaning on me. We both almost fell—but I was able to hold us up. I'd never had to before, and if Dad was healthy, I never could have.

Ann's eight.

I'm ten.

Mom and Dad are in their mid-thirties.

They never tell us. Dad dies little by little, day by day. Right in front of our eyes. And a mist of lies obscures the truth.

I wonder if they regretted their decision. Even for a moment.

I have—ever since.

Thinking back, those letters from Mayo Clinic said a lot I didn't understand at the time.

Mom almost came right out and said that she'd just about had it—she couldn't stand having to stay put when all she could think about was the two us back in Kokomo. As faint as they were, all our hopes of Mom and Dad returning home in time for Christmas were dashed on the 22nd. *I'm not sure what kind of a Christmas I'll have,* Mom wrote. *I'll be mixed up, but you know me—I'm always that way.*

She was trying to find Dad a sweater and happy that we had Christmas all planned. She was proud of how Ann and I had handled ourselves and for understanding the whole situation.

Mom called us on the 23rd. Long distance was expensive in those days, so this was a big deal. In her letters, she'd said she wouldn't call us until she knew for sure when they were coming home, but they weren't leaving yet. Dad had told her that she could come home by herself for Christmas, but she was staying with Dad.

Christmas Eve's letter doesn't say when Mom and Dad are planning to leave for Kokomo—nor Christmas's, nor the day after that. In her letter on the 27th, Mom says the big day has finally arrived: *Today the doctors told Dad he could leave tomorrow if nothing else went wrong.*

The letter's postage was ten more cents than what was required for first class delivery. "Special Delivery" was written on the envelope in Mom's handwriting. We figured this might've meant something, but we weren't sure. Maybe we were afraid to guess.

I remember what happened next like it was yesterday. Ann and I anxiously sat at the kitchen table with Mom's letter still in the envelope. Christmas was over and we hadn't received word of when our parents would return. We thought having Dad back at home would fix everything, not knowing that what had been broken could never be fixed.

As she stared at the envelope, Ann began crying. "I miss

them so much," she said.

It was all I could do to keep from crying myself. If I hadn't been concentrating so hard on opening the stubborn envelope, I probably would have. "I miss them too," I told her.

"I'm scared!" Ann said.

I felt my chest tighten in the beginnings of an asthma attack as I managed to tear the envelope open. My first cough coincided exactly with my unfolding the letter.

Ann came and stood over my right shoulder so we could read together. It didn't take long for us to find the good news. "THEY'RE FINALLY COMING HOME!" we shouted in unison.

I was happy, but my chest felt like it was in a vise. "It sounds too good to be true," I said, my voice a hoarse whisper. Ann had stopped crying. "But Mom says they'll be here. She wouldn't lie to us!" she exclaimed.

We reread Mom's letter, thinking the words might change upon closer examination, but they didn't. "I don't think she would," I said. "It says here that they'll be able to leave tomorrow afternoon if nothing else goes wrong."

"Well... did it?" Ann said, puzzled.

"Dummy! There's no way for us to know that from the letter," I shot back impatiently.

"Did you have to call me THAT?" she whined.

It suddenly dawned on me that I had goofed. "I'm really sorry," I mumbled as I looked at the letter again. "It—it says she's made reservations just in c-case —*cough*— they'll be coming. *Cough*. She'll call us if there are. *Cough*. If she doesn't c-call—"

My asthma was shifting into high gear.

As if Mom was reading our minds, the telephone rang. We leaped up and rushed into the next room to hear Mom's voice say, "WE'RE COMING HOME!" She sounded like she was in the room with us.

The following afternoon, Ann and I stood on the platform at the train station. Straining her neck to look off in the distance, Ann saw a speck approaching, growing larger. "They're almost here," she mumbled as if not believing it herself. "THEY'RE ALMOST HERE!" she shouted, jumping up and down with excitement.

I stood on the platform and coughed, afraid to look toward the train; I'd already learned that disappointment was far too frequent an occurrence in life. The engine came to a slow stop at the platform, and the cars opened. Dad was the first to get off, his steps measured and tentative as if uncertain of his footing. Mom followed closely behind, ready to help Dad if the need arose. Dad's arms reached out to embrace us, and we hugged him in return.

When our parents left for Rochester, we were truly one family. But by deciding not to tell us what really happened on their trip, that whole was shattered into pieces. Pieces held together by lies. Pieces that could move and form patterns, but never again form a whole.

And I would soon learn that hope is nothing but a contrivance—a patterned reflection—of our illusions.

Chapter 5

Uncle Mike never saw me play for the Nationals. At twenty-five, he was starting a family of his own, so he didn't have a chance to make it to the park. I remember Mike from years before that, playing football in the street with his friends. He was in his teens and hadn't left my grandparents' home yet. I'm standing off to the side, watching on the sidewalk. I was too small to join them—and that made me envious. But I knew things would change. *Someday I'll be big enough to do this too,* I thought.

The sun is always shining in these recollections, and I'm sweating because it's hot.

This was right about the time I became interested in playing sports. As hard as I try, I can't remember Dad ever being a part of this—my first awkward efforts at throwing a football, shooting a basketball, or holding a baseball bat in my hands. All my memories of my dad from back then are of him being under the weather—for a variety of reasons—and having to stand on the sidelines. Somehow I managed to teach myself.

Much later, after Dad was gone, I started playing home run derby every Fourth of July with Mike. We played with a Whiffle ball and real bats. It was always hot then, too. In Little League I hit for average, but by now I had plenty of power. I won most of those intense contests, I think—but these memories are becoming more and more hazy.

Later on, I played basketball with my other uncles, Steve and Norman. Both tried their best to outmuscle me—tried, but failed. I easily beat them.

They're all gone now.

But if this is really the case, why am I seeing these images of Mike flickering through the windshield in front of me? His ghost and no others; his alone, and there's no mistaking it.

I still can't believe he's dead.

He had heart problems for as long as I can remember, but this morning's phone call still hit me like a brick right between the eyes. When did I talk to him last? It had to be… a month or so ago. That's when he called unexpectedly just to check in and see how my family and I were doing. I never suspected this would be the last time I'd hear his voice.

Mike's ghost is the least painful of all those who haunt me. This is a surprise, given how he'd proclaimed my atheism would send me straight to hell and that he saw no way for me to avoid that fate. By contrast, the rest of the family allowed for the possibility that I'd see the light and change my mind when I grew up.

But like any rational man having irrational experiences, I'm finding that I'm kidding myself, and the voices are nothing more than a soundtrack to a scary movie playing in my head. Seeing Mike's images through the windshield is tough for me, but at least it's keeping the others at bay. How long will I be able to hold them off? Not long.

Mike would be sixty-five if he were alive today. I'm fifty-one and still living.

Uncle Mike's ghost is gone, and now there's an eleven-year-old version of me riding my bicycle just ahead of the car. I slow down and pull over. However crazy it seems, I don't want

The Announcers

to run myself over. But no sooner do I stop and park by the curb than me on the bike stops too.

It feels real, even though I know it isn't. I'm sitting on my old bicycle, eleven years old, my first lefty glove hanging down from the handlebars. I know I'm on my way to try out for Little League. It's the second day, and I'm riding to the park by myself. But that glove...

It was my first lefty glove. Freshly bought for me by Dad at Snepp & Fager's sporting goods store. I remember going there with him... Soon after he returned from Minnesota...

Talk about having the wool pulled over my eyes. When we met Mom and Dad at the train station, I felt their return that would fix everything that had gone wrong, and once we got home, I continued deluding myself into believing everything was okay. We had a late Christmas that possessed a momentum of its own; Mom and Dad even gave me a microscope, which was no small present back then. After that it was a return to "business as usual" and, for me, the fifth grade. "How did your Christmas vacation go?" my teacher asked me. I failed to notice either the tone of her question or its unusual urgency.

During his first week back, Dad appeared to tire easily, but that was all. "Nothing out of the ordinary for having a big operation," Mom explained. There was something else that couldn't be swept under the rug—something that made its presence known to all of us whether we wanted to know or not: the bag at Dad's side.

We were told it was the "brand-new plumbing they had to put in."

Mom elaborated as best she could, trying to conceal her discomfort at even addressing the topic. Ann and I nodded our heads, but we didn't really understand what it meant.

As if to reinforce the bag's closeness with Dad's life, it even had a name—Murgatroid, or "Murgy" for short. This was supposed to be funny, though I don't ever remember anyone laughing about it when Dad was alive. He was constantly cracking jokes about it, calling it his "best friend," saying that "they didn't sell any of these babies in a common, garden-variety store." No one laughed at these jokes either.

In fact there were more than a few tears shed over Murgy, since it was a very real presence in our lives that never went away. This was particularly true on those days when Dad had what was referred to as one of his "accidents" in the bathroom.

Mom and Dad were doing their very best to put on a show for Ann and me. They managed to pull off their little charade fairly well under the circumstances. This was made easier because I was wearing blinders, wanting everything to be back to normal more than anything in the world.

Even in those early days there were times Dad felt truly rotten. All we could do was hunker down and cross our fingers that whatever was happening would shortly pass. There was seldom any warning. Ann and I would suddenly find ourselves caught in the crossfire of pain and sharp words. Then everything had to be explained away, cloaked in a web of lies concealing the reality staring us in the face—

"Things will quickly get back to normal. Everything's okay," Mom would tell Ann and me reassuringly while Dad remained silent. I don't think either one of us heard the desperation that must have been creeping into her voice. I wanted the words to be true, so I let them be true.

Although we didn't know it, we were already a world apart from the other residents of Kokomo. We were in our own little club, and everyone else was secretly relieved that they weren't members.

Cancer wasn't leprosy, but it wasn't openly mentioned in polite society. It was a word that shocked and offended and might even be contagious. These were Christian folk. Obviously we had done something wrong—otherwise, in the eyes of many of our neighbors, this "divine" judgment wouldn't have been visited upon us.

I carry the burden of my parents' lies, but given the circumstances, given the time and place, more than likely I would have done the same goddamn thing if I were in their shoes and lied, too. That knowledge, of course, makes me even madder.

Mom concocted a fantasy world where everything was still normal, and Dad went along with it. They spent every waking hour playacting so that no day was different from any other. They kept everything on an even keel—at the expense of all else.

Then one day in February, Dad got the bright idea it was time for me to have a baseball glove for lefties. He admitted that he'd gotten tired of me putting on Uncle Norman's right-handed glove on the wrong hand. It was awkward as hell, using the wrong glove on the wrong hand, but I'd gotten to a point where I was fairly good at it.

Without saying so, Dad was prepping me for the start of Little League season, which was a few months away. I would be eleven, which meant I had two full seasons ahead of me if I were successful.

A week or so later, Dad took me to buy my first lefty glove. When the day was over I couldn't have been happier.

Should I have been?

Chapter 6

The before day Dad took me to buy that first lefty glove started out very bad, although it was supposed to have been good. Many days started out good and ended up bad. Usually, when they began on a sour note, they stayed that way.

Mom and Dad were in the kitchen while Ann and I were in our bedrooms. Normally that would have made it harder for us to hear, but on this day it didn't make any difference. We could have been on the next block—or further away than that—and still heard.

So many of their arguments happened in the kitchen.

A lot more happened in other rooms of the house.

They must have thought we couldn't hear them.

They happened everywhere—there was no place for Ann and me to hide.

On this day, Mom's voice was quieter than Dad's and disjointed, as if she was trying to figure out what to say as she spoke. "A-are y— you feel— bet— better? T-the kids—," I think she was saying, but this is fuzzy. If all of my memories were fuzzy, maybe it'd be easier to remember this one, but unfortunately this isn't the case.

It was tougher for me to figure out what Dad was thinking or why he did what he did, though, because I was only eleven. Like what it meant when Dad raised his voice. No—shouting was what it was. Even after all these years, I definitely recall him shouting, "My guts feel as though they're being ripped apart from the inside!" I can't begin to conceive how this must have felt.

After Dad's outburst, Ann came into my room, crying. "Dad's yelling again," she said. Her words weren't a complaint but more like a plea for something to be done.

If only I could have helped.

I wanted so much to tell her she was making it all up. That way it wouldn't be happening. But she wasn't making it up. No way. And not only was it happening, it was happening to all of us—right at that very instant in a way we couldn't ignore. But I didn't say anything, which was about as awkward as anything could possibly be. And things got worse, as the argument was replaced by a silence worse than any shouting. And the silence was followed by the heavy sounds of Dad's footsteps as he rushed from the kitchen to the bathroom—

Now that I think about it, more bad things happened in the bathroom than any other room in the house.

And this was about to be one of the worst.

Mom suddenly came into my room to ask us to either stay where we were or go into the living room to watch television. She wasn't telling us—she was begging us—but we didn't listen. We had to be with Dad—we had to be with him because we sensed something terrible was happening to him and maybe we could help.

Maybe.

Because—

Dad was in desperate flight to the bathroom—fleeing in order to avoid having shit and blood gush from the hole in his side and spill onto the floor or whatever else.

The Announcers

Whatever else—

Even the smallest memory scraps retain their sting quite nicely; the sharp pain associated with re-hearing, re-seeing, and re-smelling what occurred on that Friday before Ann and I went to school and Dad hadn't gone to work—

All simultaneously—

It's still so sharp—so clear—like a shard of glass slicing my cheek—

Mom's "Oh God!"—and the sound—the gushing sound—before the sight—the sight of—of IT—all starting to gush out—and almost as fast, like a tidal wave—the smell, the HORRIBLE smell—making me gag—gagging—blinded—wanting to throw up—needing to vomit—but where—into—into—into all the blood and—and and and—that black churning mass—Dad's—his—the bag couldn't hold it—couldn't—it just—kept coming—gushing out—like a dam had burst—like a—a—lake of shit—exploding—did it—did some of it get on my hands—did—did it—it caught me—caught me by—complete surprise. Everything—was happening all at once—"Oh God!"—happening so fast that Dad dumped what remained in the bag into the bathroom sink—I can see the lines in his closed eyes—his hands clenched—knuckles white—trying to hold the bag over the hole in his side—trying to catch what was gushing out—out of that hole—that void—oozing shit and blood—it held—still holds—my eyes prisoner—"Oh God!"—maybe there was vomiting?— maybe I did vomit—nothing Dad could do was working—but then—the gushing and oozing—the sounds, the horrible sounds— suddenly stopped—and the mess—all the blood and shit—mixed together—a hellish sludge—like a painting—of death—shit and blood and death all over—"OH GOD!"—death in the sink, on the floor, on the walls, on his hands, on his clothes—

J. G. Perkins

"OH GOD!"—death all over everything—"OH GOD!"—all over, all over, all over, all over all over all over all over all over—

    I looked at my hands, my clothes. Were they... still clean?

    I don't remember.

    Mom began tidying up.

    Something stirred in my lungs. My chest—

    "Please go and watch TV," she said to Ann and me.

    I felt dizzy.

    "Wash yourself and go lie down," she said to Dad.

    My chest   began   to...   to tighten...

*   my chest feels funny i don't want to go and watch tv i go to my room to be alone and begin to cough he's not yelling for me to hear cough   cough   he's always yelling at us he doesn't mean to is what mom always says i'm afraid i'm going to be sick again*

*   i want to feel safe*

*   i never do except when i'm under all my blankets at night it's too hot for me to do that now but i'm going to   anyway*

*   mom won't be mad at me if i do   cough   cough   he's still not yelling*

*   i guess   i   i   couldn't take it after awhile what i saw things got real blurry all of a sudden cough*

*   i had to look away*

*   i won't leave any of the blankets out   all those in the closet on top of the ones already on   my bed and the pillows i put under the sheet on both sides of me for added protection*

The Announcers

    nothing can get at me   noth—

    cough   cou—

    getting the blankets out   and the pillows   and arranging them   is making me feel better alreadyeach one in its proper place so i can crawl beneath and within to feel safe

    this is the only way

    crawling in and snuggling inside where it's   so   hot but not as hot as out there   it could burn me up   it almost did

    now it's good   i can't hear him yell   what i saw hasn't gone away but it's dark   dark   dark and this is making it get dimmer

    dark and more dark has settled in all around me   even better it's making all the bad stuff i saw   go away   my chest feels better

    the rest of me does too better and better the longer i'm snuggled in

    i'll stay here and never go back out

    never

    mom could bring me food   here   i could reach my hand out and bring it back in   she wouldn't have to see me   this would work   yes   really work except   no darn it   she will never let me do this   no use asking so   so   i'll have to pretend that   the blankets and pillows surround me   when i'm outside

    no one will be able to see them

J. G. Perkins

    this is what i'll do   to stay safe

    i'll try it   right now   i'll go back   into the living room

    picturing   pillows and blankets   surrounding   me

    dad is feeling much better   he's all washed up
the house is   back in shape   everything is as far
as i can tell   i feel the blankets around me   even though
they're invisible no one sees them   and they're protecting me from
everything   at least for now   even supper when dad
yells the most   but he's not yelling   he   must be tired

    mom is really cheerful

    ann and i are on our best behavior   this is tough for her

    she never behaves   but we pull it off

    night is here   i go back to my room   my real blankets and pillows   dark is better than light   there's no sound and no bad dreams   dark is better when there's nothing

    suddenly i wake up   it's light   but i don't want it to be
        a new day   saturday   no school   dad would be
at work   making tire weights but he's home   why   is he
sick all over again   but

    mom and dad are laughing

    they're acting like   nothing happened   before
nothing as bad as what happened   really bad   about
as bad as it could get

    i'm trying to forget   what happened   but i'm trying to forget what

    and from the kitchen he's yelling   at me   no   it's

The Announcers

not yelling but   him talking louder   so i can hear   talking louder and telling me   to bring my baseball mitt to him

*   dad always calls it a mitt when i call it a glove   it was my uncle's   and it's a righty   but i'm a lefty   turned it upside down so it would fit   it took me a long time to get used to it but i've done it*

*   what does dad want with it*

*   c-coming   i'm saying   before i know it   my voice doesn't want to work but does   my legs don't want to move but they do   i'm afraid to go into the kitchen because he's there   i don't know what he wants   now mom's peeking her head through the door   she's smiling   don't be shy she's telling me you have a big surprise in store*

*   a surprise?*

*   i want to be happy as i walk into the kitchen   but i see dad looking down   at his side   at murgy   the very same place that   only yesterday   why is he doing that i'm confused   again*

*   something must be wrong   again   cough wheeze   terribly wrong   but*

*   hurry hurry he's telling me   we have an errand we have to do downtown   hurry hurry   his voice isn't hurting like it was yesterday   it sounds really excited i don't know the last time i heard it sound this way*

*   now i'm asking him   what we're going to do   i feel like i really have to know   but don't know why*

*   come on   he's saying   get the lead out you'll see soon enough dad's joking with me*

J. G. Perkins

he almost never jokes   why now   if only he doesn't look at his side   again where   that bag   is joking   but   i'm afraid to laugh

*   mom laughs for me   have a good time you two*

*   ann is asking why she can't go*

*   mom tells her dad is buying a baseball glove for me   she'll be getting something special when   we get back*

*   dad and i are alone   together   in our new light blue ford*

*   alone together   without mom and ann   it's really making me antsy*

*   i know we're headed downtown   he's already told me that but i don't know where downtown   we're about halfway there but still he hasn't told me so i'm asking if he's ever going to tell me where we're headed*

*   no*

*   his voice sounds like a drum pounding   no no no no no no   no no no*

*   he's not going to say   he's telling me to be patient because i'll see soon enough   how soon   i think   if only i was brave enough to ask*

*   i'm wearing my glove the wrong way on my hand   just like i always have to wear it why did you want me to bring this i ask it feels like it's a part of my hand   i could never imagine it not being there whenever i wanted it to be*

*   your glove's getting kind of old*

*   dad's voice is not a drum but*

glove getting kind of old   i hadn't thought of that before   maybe   i answer

he's thinking   a little bit   before claiming   i've likely about worn my mitt out   here he goes with his thing about mitt again   only catchers wear mitts but i'll never tell him that

i'm holding my glove up real close to my eyes   it doesn't have much padding

but   i've sort of gotten used to it   the way it fits on my hand

the drum of dad's voice returns   does that include turning it over so your fingers will fit into it

he already knows the answer to this   he has to

yes   he's seen me do it

his voice is softer now asking whether this makes it hard to catch the ball

we're practically downtown now   wherever dad and i are going has to be close by

n-no not really not as hard as it was at first I don't miss many catches anymore   i say   in a big rush   like there won't be time to finish

but he wouldn't know because he never plays catch with me some day he's always saying to me that he will   but he never looks me straight in the eye when he says it

now i can barely hear him talk   with all the wind rushing through the window   isn't it about time for little league tryouts i think he says   and   someone mentioned that to me the other day

J. G. Perkins

he forgets who it was

i think so   little league tryouts   i mean   i haven't given it much thought one way or the other   dad's voice is beginning to sound strange while he tells me that i'm almost eleven and   i'd have two full seasons ahead of me   stranger than i've ever heard it

i'm thinking that's right   if i was good enough to ever make a team just thinking it and all at once i hear myself say it

the wind through the window is really picking up blowing in real hard   but not enough to keep dad from advising me that   i shouldn't be so down on myself because he's watched me play

he's watched me play and thinks i have a good arm and a nice swing

i   never knew this   never ever   he's saying he thinks i'd stand a pretty good chance if i tried out   i'm getting really excited   does he really think so

the wind stops blowing and we get out of the car   we're walking and i still have my glove on my hand

we don't have far to go now   dad's saying   where we're going is just around the corner not much further to go at all

he isn't going to tell me   not even now when we're just about there

we're walking along and dad's still talking   asking me whether i said a while back that with my righty glove turned around i rarely missed a ball

i remember saying that just a minute ago but before i can

The Announcers

answer he stops me on the sidewalk   stops and turns me around   he almost falls over but doesn't   why   nothing's hit him   now i'm facing him   just think what you could do with a lefty   he says

   i'm looking   at my upside-down righty   now   yeah i'm saying yeah   but i don't know for sure because i've   gotten kinda used to this one

   he's looking at me funny   i don't understand why   he's looking at me this way   okay he says   but wouldn't a lefty glove be a whole lot more comfortable

   i don't know

   i don't—

   we're walking around a corner   well son you're about to find out

   we've turned the corner and i see snepp & fager's it's my favorite sporting goods store   why have we come here   i ask

   you'll see soon enough   he says

   we walk in and a salesman greets dad   hi i'm frank what can i do for you he says to dad   and dad points to me and says my boy needs a lefty mitt to replace the righty he's wearing on the wrong hand   why is he saying this   glove not mitt i'm thinking again but before i speak up i hear frank's very loud HELLO YOUNG MAN   i say hi

   we're walking to where the baseball gloves are   i've never seen so many   dad puts his hand on my shoulder   why now he almost never touches me   why now   frank's talking again   well you've come to the right place young man what do you have in mind   a replacement glove for the one you have   his voice sounds like we're at a carnival

67

J. G. Perkins

    i'm looking at my righty glove for what might be the last time it doesn't want to come off my hand   but it finally does   i'm giving it to my father and he takes it from me

    i can no longer see it although i'm trying very hard

    i wish i had it back but i'm not saying this aloud   i'm speaking in sputters   no in stutters   no   i-i-i need a glove that really fits my right hand

    the carnival man   frank   is almost yelling YOU'RE A LEFTY YOU THROW LEFT- HANDED   right   maybe you're even the next whitey ford   do you follow the yankees

    how did he know   that's my favorite team   sure do my favorite player is mickey mantle

    frank's nodding back at me   THE MICK   mine too let's see what we have for you

    dad's somewhere off to the side   i can't see him or my old glove frank is going through the stack of gloves on the table   he's picked four out

    i can't help but hear him since he's standing next to me   here we are   a good selection try 'em on to see how they fit you

    wow finally a glove that feels the way it should

    i'm taking time to test   all four lefty gloves   dad's suddenly beside me too and i show him each one   he doesn't say anything he only nods after he sees each glove

    not the mitts this time   he finally knows i'm not a catcher

    one of the gloves feels really good   too good to be true this is the glove i want   now dad is nodding his head in approval i take a baseball from the table to really test it out i toss and catch the ball in the glove over and over and over

no doubt about it   this is the one   it has a really good feel

dad asks if i'm really sure   he hands my old glove to carnival frank

YES

i've never been this excited   on the spur of the moment i take three or four steps away from dad i take the baseball out of my new glove and throw it to him

here CATCH!

it should be easier than a can of corn   only it's not

he's taken by complete surprise   which only explains part of what i see   he drops the ball on the floor after coming nowhere close to catching it   i don't believe what's happening

dad's embarrassed   i can tell   i missed it he says   he rubs his eye   he's making an excuse   something must have been in my eye   i look there but only see something i don't understand   something that scares me

m-my   fault   s-s-sorry   i'm   stuttering again somehow i get control of myself   i should have given you more warning

frank's voice is much quieter   much more serious   pay no attention to the baseball no big deal i'll get it later   he hands me another baseball so i can put it in my glove

dad is trying to act as though nothing has happened   he's talking and i'm trying to listen   are you sure it's the glove you

J. G. Perkins

want no one's pressuring you   his voice is shaky

   i feel nothing but pressure

   nothing

   i don't like anything about this and i'm not understanding the reasons why   but i can't say anything about it   i have to do and say something though   so   i take the baseball i just got out of my glove   and   look at dad and put the baseball back in the glove   yes it's the one   i say without stuttering while looking at the three gloves i don't want

   now i'm holding up my right hand with the glove and baseball

   this is DEFINITELY the one

   dad's voice is almost as loud as carnival frank's was

      WE'LL TAKE IT

   carnival frank is telling me that i made such a good choice that the mick would approve   that he'll even throw in the baseball as a bonus

   all i can manage to say is thank you   i feel a whole lot more needs to be said but don't know how to say it

   dad's voice booms   THANK YOU

   the booming in my ears doesn't go away

   dad and i walk out   of snepp & fager's without saying anything to each other   the new

      glove and baseball are still   on and in my hand   we're walking on the street back to the car now   my chest is starting to tighten but i'm not coughing   good   but   something's troubling me   a voice inside my head says i shouldn't say it out loud to dad   that i would regret it later   but before i can catch myself   i   hear   my   own voice

The Announcers

    dad   c-can I ask you s-something

    where's the wind when you need it   the wind's not blowing
anywhere   *maybe he didn't hear me*   maybe
i hope not

    but   dad does   *he does and instead of wind i
hear*   sure son the sky's the limit   *i want his voice to be back
to normal but i'm not sure that it is*   i want to run and
hide   *but i'm trapped*   i've trapped myself so that i have to
sputter   w-why d-d-did you miss m-m-my throw just now b-back
in snepp & fager's

    but maybe i don't want to hear the answer

    we suddenly stop on the sidewalk   i don't want to stop but we
do

    before dad answers he taps his side where murgy is   i don't
think he realizes he's doing it   *i want to look away but don't*
he drops his hand to his side   *he pauses and asks*   what
do you mean exactly

    his voice still isn't normal but it's different than what it was
   higher sounding in a way   *i'm making him mad*   i try
never to make him mad   *but*   i'm always messing up

    i started this so i have to explain myself   try to explain
myself so   when i tossed you the ball back there   *not making
myself clear* so   *remember i tried to throw*

    so you would have an easy time catching it   *still
not clear*   so   how could you miss when it was coming
right at you

    i'm really blowing this in a big way   and to make matters
worse dad's not   saying anything

 much worse people are walking around us and looking back as they do how awkward can things get all of a sudden we're the star attractions when i wish i could say a magic word and disappear from everyone's view

 he's still not saying anything and i'm having to look down at the sidewalk

 the sun's bearing down on me it's getting to be real hot and before i know it i'm hearing dad's voice it sounds like an announcer on tv i never heard him talk this way before

 it's really weird as i'm listening listening to dad and having to hear

 any five-year-old could have handled that one with their eyes closed CLUMSY CLUMSY CLUMSY it caught him off-guard folks and he dropped it like a rookie no doubt that it was the biggest flub imaginable no lie sports fans belongs in the record books a monumental error FATHER E–FATHER write it down an error no doubt about it ABSOLUTELY NONE the scorekeeper needs to write it down before we play the rest of the inning now his son is asking to explain it away to explain why his father dropped a throw he should have been able to catch in his sleep does anyone out there in the listening audience happen to have a good reason handy other than

 dad's not finishing

 all of sudden we start walking so fast it's hard for me to keep up

 we get in the car and drive back home i'm carrying my new glove and baseball in both hands as soon as we walk through the door ann points to me and asks mom and dad why did HE get a present when i haven't gotten anything

The Announcers

  i love my new glove   but as ann's talking i'm looking at dad's face and   cough   wheeze   his face is showing something   i don't   understand and

 i don't   cough   it's bothering me almost as much as it did before when i had to look away when he was standing   by the basin   in the bathroom   and murgy   was

 ann won't go away   is it because i'm a girl and he's a boy   is it

 mom pulls a new doll out of her purse and hands it to ann here you are IT'S YOURS i was waiting for your brother and father to get home so we could surprise you

 ann's making a face

 anoooooother doll

 dad's face is different but not any better

 you don't like it

 i threw the ball so it would hit him in the middle of his chest i'm thinking   cough   perfect strike if there ever was one

 mom is holding up the doll so ann can see it better

 it's not just any ordinary humdrum doll   IT'S A BARBIE

 and dad's saying

 you don't have one like this   your mother and i checked to make sure

 ann says she doesn't know

 but she should because mom's telling her that she doesn't and dad worked very hard to be able to buy it AND it's absolutely the very best they make

J. G. Perkins

ann's looking at the doll   it's okay i guess   i'm beginning to like her   i'll name her annie   that way her name will sound like mine

the only thing dad told me that made any sense was that something got in his eye

but i knew   i could tell   there was something   else

i wouldn't have thrown the ball if i'd known   never in a million years

Chapter 7

Somehow I'm outside of the car now, standing frozen on Market Street. The ballpark feels like it's light years away, but the eleven-year-old version of me is just twenty feet ahead, riding around on my old bike. He looks like he's getting fidgety. I can remember that feeling, waiting to ride to the park before tryouts and practice. Right now, though, my feet seem to be glued to the pavement, and the seasons are suddenly going in reverse. I can feel spring in the air, and the houses look just like they did back in '50s. Everything is neat and tidy. If I didn't know I was awake, I'd swear I was in one of those dreams I had after Dad died.

Watching him—me—go 'round in circles is taking me back to Little League tryouts. It was a total fluke I even went out for baseball at all. After Dad's less-than-subtle mention of tryouts during our trip to Snepp & Fager's, I filed it away at the back of my mind until the actual day arrived. This was when the "fluke" showed up: a neighbor boy came to our door. He wanted to try out but didn't know how to get to Northside. I knew the way, though, and agreed to take him there the next morning—and just like that, I'd decided to try out myself.

Up until then, my ball-playing abilities were the furthest thing from my mind, but suddenly I couldn't wait to tell my father. At first I couldn't figure out why I was so eager to tell him, but I quickly figured it out. Baseball was incredibly important to Dad, and the only thing more important than the sport itself would be watching me play it.

Later in the day, Dad came home from work and settled

into his smoking chair. I approached him cautiously, the butterflies in my stomach swirling worse than a Kansas twister. I was unsure if I had the courage to tell him about my new plan. Fortunately, a good idea struck me, and I grabbed my new glove and ball from my room and came back, stopping between Dad and the television, where I started tossing the ball in the air and catching it. I was trying my very best to smile.

After what felt like a couple hundred tosses, I caught the ball one last time then blurted out the news. "Little League tryouts at Northside tomorrow at 10:00 am," I said. I fingered the ball uneasily as I studied his face, trying to gauge his reaction. It took all the courage I had. But all Dad did was sit there like a bump on a log. The butterflies in my stomach fluttered even more. I had to say something else—anything! As a last resort, I started telling Dad about the neighbor boy who wanted to try out too, and I found myself getting excited for the first time.

"Maybe—maybe—maybe it'd be—a good idea—if I went out there with him—to help him out," I said, hastily starting and stopping like a new driver learning how to change gears. "It wouldn't hurt anything. And it'd—it'd also be a good chance to give my new glove a workout. And… and… and… it's on the way to Grandma and Grandpa's house and it's real easy to find." I didn't mention the real reason I decided to do it—that it would please him.

Whatever I said did it, because Dad sort of erupted from his chair. "GREAT! THAT'S THE SPIRIT! HAVE AT 'EM!" he said excitedly, his voice practically blasting through the roof. After this, he settled down and sat back in his chair without taking his eyes off me. "If you ask me," he said, his voice calm now, "it's considerably more than a simple 'maybe.' Next to a sure thing if there ever was one."

Sometimes the way Dad talked went over my head, and he must've picked up on it this time. "Your new glove should give you an advantage, especially with a coach," he explained. "It'll provide you with an extra edge. Yes indeed, it'll make a real difference. I know you have it in you to make the team."

"Gee, Dad," I said, uncertain, "do you really think so? There'll be a lot of other kids out there better than me."

"Don't say that!" Dad urged. "I've been… watching you play." His voice was suddenly sad.

I guess he saw me look back at the floor and knew what I was thinking: he'd watched me play, but he wasn't able to play himself. I immediately felt sorry for thinking this, and Dad must have sensed my shame, because he had trouble with what he said next—hesitating, groping for his words, and—I was too young to appreciate this at the time, but it's coming in clear now—struggling to express the immense pride he felt deep inside.

"I… I think you have all it takes," he said, his eyes gleaming. "And if you make it, we'll go back to Snepp & Fager's to buy you real baseball shoes. Shoes with metal cleats just like in the big leagues."

"REALLY?" I said, totally surprised. "Just like Mantle's? That'd be great!" And, as if to seal the deal in my own mind before chickening out, I exclaimed, "I'LL DO IT!! I'LL TRY OUT!!"

I wish this was where this bunch of memories stopped—I'd keep it apart from all the rest and be able to cherish it the way

I want. But then, none of my memories are free from the pain of what came afterward—not one. To possess just one memory that wasn't tainted would be truly special. I'd give almost anything to know how that feels.

I threw my ball into the air three times, catching it each time. "My new glove feels really *good!*" I said. As I continued tossing the ball up and down, Dad struggled to get up from his chair. "Throw me the ball again!" he said in a strange voice.

Those butterflies flew the coop, and I felt sick to my stomach. Suddenly Mom was standing at Dad's side. The expression on her face told me more than her mouth could possibly say, but she went ahead and spoke anyway. "NO!" she reprimanded. "Once is enough. Don't put yourself—and him—through this for a second time. Haven't you had enough?"

I was nervous and wanted all of this to go away. I threw the ball into the air again but dropped the catch. I left the ball on the ground, hoping Dad would listen to Mom and give up, but Dad held fast. He was staring at me, not blinking, waiting for my toss. "Are y-you sure y-y-you w-want me to?" I stammered.

"I'll be certain to keep my eyes on it this time," Dad promised. "No problem. Not a single one." There was no way I could avoid throwing him the baseball now. All I could do was give him the perfect toss—the softer, the better.

I glanced at Mom. Her face was distorted into something almost impossible to describe, like hopelessness and helplessness melted together into one pitiful, bitter shape. I wished I'd never see that face again—I wish it didn't haunt me now—but the future wasn't in the business of taking requests.

The Announcers

Dad put his hands up in front of his chest. He was ready. He starting talking in slow motion: "Yes... throw it... hit... the... old... target..." And before I knew it, the voice I was hearing sounded just like it did when we were standing on the sidewalk outside of Snepp & Fager's. It was his announcer's voice! "Two outs, bases loaded, one-run lead, and we're in the bottom of the seventh. THE GAME DEPENDS ON THIS CATCH!"

"Do I have to?" I asked meekly.

Dad turned off his announcer's voice, but he still didn't sound normal. "Come on! Chuck it in here—right on down the fat part of the plate. The game will be ours, and we'll be sure winners!"

There was no turning back now, and I was more afraid than ever that Dad would drop this toss just like the last one. Fear hounded me; my body trembled. It seemed like my entire life depended on what I did in the next several seconds—*the next several seconds!*

"O-okay," I muttered, my mouth barely moving.

The moment overtook all of us. I could feel Mom radiating tension like an open oven on full blast. Dad's hands were tense, contorted like steel traps ready to spring shut at the slightest touch, but his glare was worse. He stared straight at me. His lips were pursed.

I began winding up like a pitcher so Dad would have plenty of warning. *Aim directly for the glove and lob it to him,* I thought. I'd never concentrated so hard. My body and arm suddenly sprang into motion. All at once the ball was out of my hand and on its way to Dad. As it flew toward him, I felt a brief pang of hatred— everything was beyond my control and I couldn't stand it. Time crawled. I closed my eyes, picturing Dad dropping the ball, and invented reasons why in my head—*I'm sorry, Dad, I threw the ball too hard, my aim was bad, I choked, I'm sorry Dad I'm sorry I'm—*

THWACK!

This sound—I'll never forget this sound. The ball had hit Dad's glove hard. I opened my eyes and looked. He'd caught it!

Dad grabbed the ball with his free hand and gripped it like he was trying to burst a pimple. His face transformed, slowly, into a grin. I'll never forget this grin either. The thwack and the smile go hand in glove with one another.

The first "tryout" was done. I'd made the cut.

So had Dad.

Chapter 8

My memories skip ahead a few days—it's tryouts for real. I'm on the field with the coach. Just the two of us. There's no chance to be nervous—too much is happening all at once. This is the first time I'm front and center on a real baseball field with fences, infield, and backstop. Not exactly Yankee Stadium, but a big deal for me. It feels huge.

Before I know it I'm at the plate, waiting for a pitch from the coach standing on the pitcher's mound. The plate is all there is—the batter's box isn't marked with chalk, so I have to imagine it. The bat is like the one I have at home; it feels really good in my hands. The pitch comes at me as big as a grapefruit, so I don't miss. Solid contact's the key. That and line drives. Hitting has always been easy for me, and I pound pitch after pitch.

The coach says "Good job!" and steps off the mound, waving me to the outfield. I run to center field as fast as my legs will carry me.

The coach is yelling at me to get ready. He calls me "Number 7" and shouts that he's going to hit me some easy flies. I'm supposed to catch them and fire the ball to him like I'm trying to throw a runner out charging from third.

The butterflies are picking up speed again. My gut says *everything* is on the line.

Crouching in an outfielder's position with my hands on my knees, I shout "READY!" The coach hits me several easy fly balls. I catch each one with ease, throwing the balls back to the coach as hard as I can. He has to dodge them to keep from getting hit.

I'm doing good. Much better than I expected, and not bad at all considering no one showed me how to do any of this—especially Dad...

The coach is yelling at me again. "WOW! GREAT EFFORT, Number Seven! You nailed those throws and got the runner at home. You might even have the arm to be a pitcher. Ready for some tough ones? I'm gonna make you run!" Every muscle in my body tenses. "Ready?"

"Ready!"

The first two fly balls he hits me are easy, and I don't have to run far. My throws to home are right on target—they'd nail any runner trying score before he'd even get near the plate. I'd never thought about it much before, but I did have quite an arm.

The coach is shouting at me. "WAY TO ZING 'EM IN HERE! WHY DIDN'T I KNOW ABOUT YOU BEFORE? WHERE HAVE YOU BEEN?"

I just shrug, glancing down at my new glove. For a second, I remember the surprise I felt when Dad told me he'd been watching me play, and the hairs on the back of my neck stand up like I'd touched a live wire.

"WELL, GREAT EFFORT!" the coach yells back. "Now for a hard one!" I breathe deep and stare at him as I hunker down, unblinking... waiting... and then, like something out of a dream—

The crack of the bat is like a gunshot—the coach's hit is solid.

The Announcers

Maybe too solid. My eyes tell me the ball is going over my head, but for some reason I take a step forward. No! I hesitate for a small eternity, and finally my legs move the right away. I'm running backwards, back to where the ball is headed... but the ball is way over my head and I'm running as fast as I can to get there... It's coming down... it's coming... and I'm running... I'm running... it's coming... but... I'm not going to be able to catch it—

I turn my head over my shoulder to look for the ball... it feels like I'm flying... like the ball is flying too... right to where I should be... if I could just... be where I should be... My glove stretches up as far as it will go... and—it's not going to beat me! I'm going to get it! It's mine! I'm going to—

When I came to, the sky was purple. Confused, I shook my head, and the sky looked normal again—that deep Indiana blue—but something was wrong. I wasn't standing—I was flat on my back, but everything was moving, almost swimming. Sitting up, I tried to look around, but the field started spinning, and my head throbbed. After a few deep breaths, I struggled to my feet and figured out what happened as best I could.

The fence was right behind me—the back of my head collided with it while I was running for the ball. But the hit was a homer. I remember steadying myself as I caught sight of the ball far beyond the fence, a bright white speck poking up from the grass spinning along with everything else. It was so bright under that summer sun it practically gleamed, taunting me like treasure out of reach, and I knew it was beyond where I should have been. I never would've gotten it.

The coach came running up to me. My head hurt worse than anything I'd ever felt, so the only thing I remember him saying is that I did well and I should stay close to the phone during the next couple of days. I wanted to believe him, but a voice in the back of my head kept telling me not to expect much. I'd failed to catch that fly ball—I might not make the team.

After my head stopped spinning, I got on my bike and went back home. Mom made a big fuss about the bump on the back of my head as soon as I walked in the door. I hadn't said a word and she hadn't even seen the back of my head, but somehow she just knew. Ann kidded me for being so clumsy, but didn't surprise me at all. Somehow her jabs boosted my confidence—other than running into the fence, I did really well at tryouts—and I felt a little better, if only for a few moments.

Mom was happy for me. "I'll keep my fingers crossed," she said as she tended to the bump. On the other hand, Ann ribbed me again about running into the fence. She was lucky Mom was in the room.

I was really looking forward to Dad coming home from work so I could tell him. The throbbing from the bump hadn't gone away, but telling Dad about tryouts was all I could think about. What would he say? I must have played out the scene of him hearing the big news at least a hundred times before he got home. He was the one who convinced me to go out for a team. Without him, I wouldn't have tried at all.

I nervously waited for Dad at the top of the stairs in the kitchen. Time seemed to stand still, but eventually I heard the car in the driveway. *HE'S HOME!* I thought. As soon as he came through the door, I charged down the stairs and blurted out some nonsense that no one would've been able to understand—something about the ball being way over my head and I knew it was a homer as soon as it left the bat but I ran for it anyways without looking where I was going and not even Willie Mays could have caught the ball but I almost did. It must have been around this time that my left hand reflexively touched the bump. I was trying to pretend that it didn't hurt, but I wasn't succeeding.

Dad was having trouble following my words, but he immediately noticed my hand. "What's wrong with your head?" he asked, alarmed, but I was too caught up in my own story and ignored his question as I continued rambling. Ann and Mom walked into the room.

"He ran into the outfield fence!" Ann interrupted. Mom chimed in and told him how she found the bump as soon as I walked through the door. I stood there, cringing, until she finished.

Afterwards, I started telling them how good I thought the tryout had been—how my hitting, fielding, enthusiasm, and even colliding with the outfield fence had wowed the coach. I could definitely tell that Dad was impressed.

A whole week passed before the call came. It was excruciating at home—all of us were on edge. Mom and Dad tried talking to me, but they didn't have the right words. One awkward attempt at conversation led to another after another until they just gave up. The whole family tried to avoid talking about the call during supper, but we did anyway, or at least until Murgy acted up and Dad had to leave the table. He went to bed early, which wasn't unusual by now.

But even as we waded through all these troubles—me waiting for a phone call with a knot in my stomach and a gigantic bump on the back of my head, Dad trying to keep things under control without being overwhelmed by Murgy, Mom trying to reassure me and keep Dad calm without breaking down, and Ann caught unawares in the middle—we held together. Even if we had no plan—no plan for how to deal with the silent phone, no plan for how to deal with Dad's pain—we had each other.

Looking back, I'm not sure that made anything better, but I don't want to imagine the alternative.

All we could do was wait.

Chapter 9

I'm still standing on Market Street, drifting in and out of memories. Nothing's changed, but I'm falling further into my recollections, remembering when the coach told me to be sure and be by the phone at home. I'm getting goose bumps thinking about it now—but painful goose bumps, and the anticipation of what's to come is making me nauseous, like every goose bump will be slit with a scalpel... and all the pieces will fragment, disintegrate, disappear... something like that happened with the scalpel they used on dad...

i couldn't think of anything else at school   not even my bruised noggin which was throbbing from the time i got to school until the time i finally went home   a phone call from northside would be coming   after i got home   i just knew it would but there was no way for me to be certain   the call   the coach said i could expect one   the call with the news about which team i'd be playing for   i didn't care which one it would be

i ran home   i was out of breath and as soon as i got through the door ann cornered me in the living room   she stuck her new doll in my face   she asked me if i wanted to see it   mom and dad gave it to me as a present she told me   like i already didn't know that   like the doll's name is annie   which i already knew too   the only new thing was ann was teaching annie to talk   what could i say except yes

i wanted to go into the dining room and sit next to the phone that way i could answer it on the very first ring and find out who i was playing for   and it'd all be over   the waiting i mean   i HATE to wait   nothing good usually comes of it   but

J. G. Perkins

for the longest time that's all i was doing while my head was still hurting   and mom asking me about every three minutes or so didn't make it any better

   during the first hour i didn't need to be anywhere near the phone because it never rang   not even once for a wrong number   mom said that was odd   the phone not ringing a single time when it should be ringing off the wall

   somehow i managed to escape from my sister long enough to run to my room and get my new glove   every night i greased it down and put my new baseball in it   then i tied it up with a rubber band to try and make a better pocket   dad said that would give me an edge

   i'd been sitting by the phone for about fifteen minutes when dad got home   i ran into the kitchen to greet him i could tell he wasn't feeling good and didn't want to show it that should have stopped me but didn't   i started telling him about not receiving the call and how much better my new glove was feeling   i had just gotten a good start when ann and annie scooted around me and stole dad's attention

   ann was saying exactly the same thing to dad as she had to me

   it took all the energy that dad had left to say that annie was very very nice   he wasn't normally this tired when he got home from work   i didn't know what was wrong

   mom was being nice when she said to ann that annie needed a rest   but her face was saying something different   something i didn't understand

   i expected ann to start pouting but she didn't   all she did was gloat at me and say okay while rocking annie in her arms until she was satisfied the doll was asleep

The Announcers

after ann left mom touched the back of my head   ouch   her touch made it hurt all over   she said the swelling hadn't gone down much if at all   but ann hadn't stayed gone long she came running back to scream at me BIG DUMMY hit the fence with your head and got a giant bump   bet it hurts

* it really does   in more ways than one   i start rubbing my head...*

...and realize I'm here, again, outside the Taurus, subconsciously rubbing my head. But it's not the pain from crashing into the outfield fence I feel—it's shock. The eleven-year-old me has returned again. Me. Again! And he's just fifteen feet away, standing in the middle of the street, looking straight at me. I want to get closer to him, but I can't move. I can feel his thoughts—our memories—taking over again. But where... where is this coming from? Where...

* dad tried to turn his face away but he didn't before i could see that it was hurting like my head was   aww leave me alone i said to ann   it's no big deal   i wanted her to evaporate   completely disappear*

* mom's face hadn't stopped saying something different when she tried to be funny by telling me that i was lucky i had a hard head and i could've broken the fence i touched the back of my head as lightly as i could and told her that it definitely got the better end of the deal*

* all of a sudden dad's voice boomed out WELL TODAY'S THE DAY*

* and then mom's much softer voice   yes   today's the day we'll find out my nerves are all in a frazzle*

* frazzle   how many times does she use this word*

J. G. Perkins

    all at once i'm the center of attention   what did the coach say to you   dad wanted to know   my mouth began to move   do we have to talk about it   i don't want to say he told me to stick by the phone

    dad came right back at me   you did have a pretty good tryout   from how it sounded the coach must have put you at the top of the list

    then ann jumped in   why would they want you

    i'm trying to ignore her   then   the phone started ringing   i was running and almost tripped

    then by the third ring i answered   i'm—straining—very—hard—to—hear—hello

    —hello—i can't hear—you   there was static on the line HELLO   the line suddenly cleared

    no   it's not   i'm afraid you have the wrong number that's okay   goodbye

    mom and dad wanted to know who it was   both saying welllll at the same time

    ann knew it was a wrong number   she started making fun of me   asking who called   i told her what she already knew and she just laughed   laughed at me really loud

    dad stopped her by making a joke   wrong number   okay wrong number there isn't a symbol for that in scorekeeping he says maybe i should make one up so we can keep track of 'em   his fingers trace the air   "wn"

    how would you like that   dad says   it happens every day i guess we take it in stride

    he looked at me to see if i approved   and i tried to laugh but

The Announcers

he had to sit down when he finished talking   he must have been feeling worse

mom said maybe it'd be better luck if someone else answered the phone next time

two wrong numbers in one day would be real unusual   dad said   in a weaker voice   but stranger things have happened   this is getting to be too nerve-racking

NO   i said   i want to answer the phone   me and   no one else

dad's eyes were closed all of a sudden   i asked him if anything was wrong and he said he was just resting them   cough   resting   them   cough

mom said it was all right for me to answer the phone   but i should cheer up   and give them time   she just knew they'd be calling   with good news   but not ann   she stuck her tongue out at me twice before retorting   no one's going to call you

SHUT UP

dad was quiet but   mom was shouting   KIDS

ann's feelings were hurt   HE TOLD ME TO SHUT UP   i thought she was gonna cry but she   didn't   i told her to shut up again

mom was trying not to be mad   goodness gracious   that's enough   be nice to one another   this is an important day for all of us

dad wasn't even trying   turning his head off to the side and speaking to none of us in particular thinking he wouldn't be heard or that we were no longer there   we're off to the races again

J. G. Perkins

it's the run-of-the-mill bickering that occurs between any brother and sister   these two included regardless of—

   but i could hear him as he went on   we all heard him

    —anything i'm doing or not doing   or murgy   the typical bill of fare for any typical household with a brother and sister   as if we fall into such a—

   we all wanted him to stop but he wouldn't

   his voice sounded like he was in a daze

    —category: "typical" i mean   i don't feel like listening to the kids squabbling   some days it grates on me more than others   and this one's proving to be off the scale   like the radio playing too loud and too long

    he paused and   his eyes relaxed slightly   *i probably feel this way because of the suspense waiting for the phone call   he said sighing   mayo's sure did a number on me*

   ann's voice joined dad's   *annie's gonna wake up*

    this time i want ann to keep talking   keep talking more than anything   but then she quickly fell silent

   mom was wringing her hands   as dad's talking took charge all over again

   mayo's made sure i would never like waiting for news again! or fail to be reminded of what news they had for me back then   if only we could find out sooner rather than later

   i   didn't understand   who was he talking about

   me   ?

   he kept going   *what's left of my gut tells me jack has a good chance but you never know   you nev—*

The Announcers

    suddenly there was a ringing in   our   ears   dad was cut off   i ran to answer as fast as i could   the bump on the back of my head began hurting   throbbing   hello   HELLO excuse me yes she's here

    i glanced at ann with daggers in my eyes and waved for her to come to the phone

    mom and dad exchanged glances

    ann yanked the phone from my hand   hello   susie hi in no time she was very excited   as excited as i wanted to be

    i'll have to ask my mother i'll call you back   goodbye she handed the phone back to me and sped over to mom

    i put the phone back down   for all i cared it could stay there

    ann was still very excited   susie wants me to come over to—

    when i interrupted and said to mom   you can answer the phone when it rings next time they're NOT going to call   you can bet on it

    mom turned away from ann and began speaking to me come on   don't get down in the dumps   the day's young yet they probably haven't got around to making the calls   give 'em a chance   they had to be impressed with you   after all you almost went through the fence running after a homer   you'll have more to show for that than just a lump on the head   trust me   you'll be getting a call

    ann interrupted my interruption   susie wants me come over to her house to play this afternoon

    mom had to turn away from me and toward dad   i don't see why she can't   can you dad acted shocked that he was having to talk   not a reason in the world   none whatsoever   i might be wrong but he couldn't have cared less about this

ann was trying to rush by me to get to the phone   rushing by me with THANKS A MILLION i'll call susie right now gushing from her mouth

WAIT   SHE CAN'T   DON'T LET HER   i was almost screaming

mom or dad needed to keep her from using the phone   right then and there with no questions asked   ann stopped in her tracks and started to pout

could you please hold off for just a little while   mom said next   why was she asking and not telling i wondered   she should have been telling   and i almost said as much   but

oh okay i'll wait 'til he gets his dumb call   ann said

gosh   thanks   i said   our latest scrap was out of the way   finally   now the table was set for me to get the call it didn't much matter what they said to me as long as i made a team ANY TEAM

i reminded mom to not forget that when the phone rang again she should answer it   then i begged her and she nodded her head that she would

we all waited without saying anything for about a minute or two   when the phone started ringing again   we all jumped like we'd been shocked   mom started off to answer the phone just like she said she would when it stopped ringing   just like that she stayed frozen in her tracks   we were all frozen

it seemed like forever but wasn't any more than thirty seconds

The Announcers

or so before the phone rang again   even louder than it did before   we all jumped again   but maybe it was another false alarm

*   a second ring followed on the heels of the first   mom leaped into action as if she was afraid that she would miss the call this could be it   she said   the call*

*   i didn't think it was though   not for a minute*

*   all our eyes were glued on her*

*   she answered   H HELLO   she was straining to hear HELLO   still straining   could you speak louder please   i can barely hear you*

*   no one could hear whoever it was   but mom did at last   although she didn't understand what was being said to her WHO   she asked   someone was on the other end of the line   i was convinced   someone   but   who*

*   mom nodded her head   she wasn't straining anymore*

*   YES   you would like to speak to my son*

*   i couldn't believe my ears   it's for you   she said me   me and no one else   ME*

*   at first i'm reluctant to go to the phone   so like an idiot i stayed put and didn't go anywhere until dad gave me a nudge go ahead   he said   the moment of truth is at hand*

*   i glanced at ann but she was looking somewhere else*

*   the moment of truth   dad had been right   for the next minute   all i can do is keep my fingers crossed   my hands are sweating   this has got to work out*

*   mom patted me on the shoulder and handed me the phone*

*   i'm afraid to talk but have to say something   hello*

 this is northside little league calling IT'S THE COACH

 hi yes this is jack lewis *the coach's voice sounded as though it was coming from a thousand miles away but i could still hear him*

 saying *you've been chosen to play for the nationals congratulations*

 saying report to the ballpark tomorrow morning at 9:30

 saying see you there

 the receiver went dead but i said THANKS *anyway*

I MADE IT

I MADE IT

 I hugged Mom, and both of us rushed over to Ann and Dad. Ann said she knew I'd make it all along. Then I looked over at Dad in his chair.

 He wasn't resting his eyes. He was asleep—

 —and now I'm awake in this reality again.

 I rub my eyes. The eleven-year-old me has disappeared, vanished as if a trapdoor opened up and swallowed him. Will he come back? I wonder, and with that wonder comes a sense of unease. Where are these hallucinations coming from?

 But now some things about the past are clear. The tragedy swirling around us, invisible to me like light deflected by gravity. And such a heaviness enclosing everything, swallowing us up like a black hole and closing us off from everyone else.

 Nothing we did could be normal.

 But now I'm here—I'm not that eleven-year-old boy anymore. And I can break free from this black hole—can't I?

Maybe I can't.

But I must.

I *will*.

Step by step, one foot following the other, building a slow rhythm against the gravity of the past—

Chapter 10

I can feel Dad's presence in the shadows of the ballpark, in the shadows of so many in-between places in Kokomo. They're his places now, the park and the city. I feel him even now, at my side, accompanying me in each step I take.

Each step is different than the last. I can only hope the park's still there.

Every time I put my new glove on during my first season, I paused to think about how natural it felt. Then I'd wonder how I ever got by with a righty glove worn on the wrong hand—an old habit my kid brain couldn't seem to quit. I finally stopped putting my glove on the wrong hand right before the start of the second season, if not just after it began, when Uncle Norman surprised me with an even better glove—one worthy of a bona fide major leaguer.

I felt sad as I put the glove Dad bought me on a shelf in the closet. Now both those gloves, like my dad, are lost to me forever. If there are any memories of him available for me to cherish, they must be up ahead, at the ballpark. Anything of Dad's I can cherish rather than dread—this is what I seek.

Now I can hear Mom trying to explain it all to my sister and me. Why Dad acted like he did, why he always seemed like he was mad at us. Her voice is so clear, it's as if she's standing right next to me—*Your father hasn't been... happy for some time. He works very hard... and doesn't always appear chipper. He's not mad at you... but angry at something else.* But now Mom's voice is shrill as she says that Dad loves us more than we could possibly understand. She's almost crying.

There's a long silence, and the dust of the memory mixes with the ice in the air on Market Street as a strange shiver passes over me.

Finally, I can hear her again. *One day,* she says, *one day you will understand. Some day—*

But when?

"WHEN?" I ask, eyes searching the clouds.

I hear Dad answer me instead. "How's your head?" His voice is suddenly so crisp it makes me jump, and I spin around, thinking someone must be playing a joke on me, but no one's there. I can't figure out if the voice was real or imagined, but it seemed to come from the direction of the ballpark—almost as though he was up there in the scorekeeper's booth, announcing again...

But Dad's question—it's the same one he asked after I'd collided with the outfield fence. Without thinking, I touch the back of my head where the bump was, even though it hadn't been there for decades.

Dad's still going. "You led with your head," he says, "just like Pistol Pete did when he ran into the left field wall..."

Pistol Pete Reiser was possibly one of Dad's favorite baseball players—partially for the stories of Pete running into outfield walls over and over, but also because I got to meet Pete when I was batboy for the Kokomo Dodgers at the end of my second Little League season. I was only half-listening to what Dad was saying that night, but he told me Pete once ran into the wall so hard he was knocked out cold, and the general manager brought in a priest to give Pete his last rites. I asked Dad what last rites were, and there was a change in his tone as he responded.

"It's something a priest says to Catholics to help them think they'll be going to heaven," he explained, bitterness seeping into his voice. I thought I'd made him mad again, but now, as I recall the memory again, I can detect some subtleties that my eleven-year-old ears missed. Trying not to feel bad, I zeroed in on heaven instead. It was something we talked about a lot in Sunday school—something that sounded too good to be true—and the more we talked about it, the more confused I became. Maybe Dad understood something I didn't.

I started to ask him a question. "Will I go to heav—?"

"NOBODY—" Dad exploded, but his words collapsed like they'd been hit with a bomb. He stopped abruptly and, as if reading my mind, calmly changed the subject. "Just pay more attention to where you're goin' when—" He paused again and looked down at me. "—when you're chasing a fly ball over your head."

"I-I will," I said. And from that moment on, I did.

My family didn't look different from the other good folks of Kokomo, but one way we were out of step was that, going back several generations, we weren't churchgoers. We only attended Grace Methodist Church as a family after my parents returned from Mayo Clinic.

Upon arrival every Sunday, Ann and I were sent to separate Sunday schools, while our parents went to "Big People's" church, as my Mom called it—which I thought was funny, though I never laughed when she said it. Neither did Dad. As best as I can recall, he never laughed at anything, if he laughed at all.

I think our sudden church attendance was Dad desperately

trying to hedge his bets with God. This was quite a change—before surgery, belief wasn't part of his intellectual makeup, nor was it at the end. So all our churchgoing was for nought.

And we never went to church again, either.

Even though it feels like the dead of winter and my nose is practically frozen solid, I can still smell that leather from long ago—the leather of my cleats. I got a new pair of shoes each season. "A little something to go along with the uniform," Dad had said. They were *real* leather baseball shoes with *real* metal cleats. "You're going to have to make your shoes spick and span before every game," Dad instructed me, handing me a brush and a box of shoe polish. "Just like in the big leagues." He didn't want me to walk onto the diamond any other way—everything had to be just right.

As I opened the box containing my first pair of cleats, Dad mentioned a certain "something else" that went along with my new shoes and Nationals uniform. I set the box down to ask what, and before I knew it, we were in the car. We drove no more than two blocks before I realized we were going to Northside.

As we drove along, just me and Dad in the Ford, I didn't say a word. The moment was too perfect—I didn't want it to pass—but we reached the park after what felt like a few seconds. "We're here," Dad said, his voice sounding more than a little strange. I looked over at him, and he cleared his throat to try and cover up. "I've got something to show you," he said. His voice was back to normal.

That "something" was the scorekeeper's box behind and above home plate. It would be Dad's home away from home when he was at the ballpark.

The Announcers

Dad and I went up the ladder, which didn't seem like much until both of us were in the scorekeeper's box—Dad was out of breath after the climb. I distinctly remember thinking that this was the second recent thing that hadn't gone off as it should have—the first being the "last rites" debacle. "Nothing's wrong," Dad assured me. "It was a steep climb."

As I waited for Dad to stop gasping and catch his breath, my attention wandered over to the field where I'd be playing baseball—and I was riveted. How neat and perfect it looked! And as if to make that view even better, Dad told me that when I wasn't down on the field, I'd be up here with him. He was going to teach me how to keep score—how to read all the symbols and understand all the ins and outs of tracking a game as it moved along. Hearing this for the first time, it sounded like magic. I couldn't imagine how it could be done and, later on, I was amazed that I learned it so quickly. "Like a duck taking to water," Dad liked to say. Even to this day, I can't hear this phrase without thinking of this experience with my dad, and I can't think of the experience without hearing his voice say the expression.

Then, to top things off, Dad turned on the loudspeaker system. It was a simple flip of a switch, but it opened up a whole new world for me. "It'll take a while for it to warm up, so don't start talking into it right away," Dad joked. But I was too awed to laugh. I wish I had, though. It doesn't seem like I ever had a second chance to laugh with Dad.

It didn't take long for the loudspeaker to warm up, maybe a minute or two. As soon as it had, Dad cleared his throat again and took the microphone in his hands. "COMING UP TO THE PLATE AND BATTING THIRD, NUMBER SIX…" he announced.

Number 6? I thought, surprised at the sound of Dad's voice over the loudspeaker. *That's my number. But why is he...*

I asked Dad what he was doing, and he told me he'd signed on to be the league's announcer and scorekeeper. "Why?" I asked. It should've been obvious to me, but it wasn't.

Dad's voice suddenly became a lot quieter and more serious. "This is where I'll be watching you play for two WHOLE summers," he said.

I wasn't sure what he was trying to say, and that made me feel uneasy. I tried to look him straight in the eye and stay calm, but my mouth started jabbering. "Y-yes. The season coming up in two weeks and the season next year. After that I'll be a teenager and too old for Little League. Then it'll be Babe Ruth baseball. That'll be really neat, won't it? Will you be the announcer there too?" I was on a roll. If only I'd kept my mouth shut, it would've been better all around.

Dad turned away from me. I couldn't tell it then, but he was having a lot of trouble. A moment passed before he regained his composure.

"Wait," he said, "aren't you hurryin' things up too much? Are you sure it's only two years?" He looked out over the infield and back at me. "Somehow my figuring's gotten out of whack. Too old that soon? Funny how I thought it had to be longer."

It wasn't just his figuring, because Dad's timing had gone all out of whack too. At least this much was clear to me, and I was suddenly bothered by it. "Dad, is something wrong?" I asked.

"No, just havin' trouble keepin' my math straight," he

The Announcers

replied.

I didn't—*couldn't*—believe it. As far as math went, Dad's brain was like a steel trap. "You've never had that problem before."

When he spoke again, I didn't recognize that his voice was struggling. Each syllable, each word was a struggle. "There's a first time for everything I guess," he said. "Even for my brain misfiring on occasion. But it's definitely two years that you'll be out here... not quite as clear for... well, let's just say, other things... What's important now is that when you're out there... playing... I'll be up here... watching you. And when other teams are playing out there... you'll be up here with me. WE'LL BE TOGETHER!"

Those were Dad's exact words, but at the time, I understood only about a quarter of what he said. By the time he'd finished, I was excited about what we'd be doing in the booth and started to tell him, but it was if Dad hadn't heard me because he picked up in the same strange place where he'd left off: "This is how it'll go for us during the two seasons... we'll say that's how much time we got for now... two seasons for sure... well, pretty sure... it's much clearer than mud... yes, that's it... this season and the next... we'll forget about any complication that might rear its ugly head... there's nothin' we need to be concerned about anyway... nothin' that amounts to a hill of blue beans."

I was more confused than ever when Dad finished, and told him so.

He said it would soon become much clearer.

Chapter 11

I'm standing in the street, and it's freezing cold and beginning to snow. During my two seasons of Little League, I never saw such weather on this street—it was always warm and muggy. With the heat and humidity in the evenings, those wool baseball uniforms could really get scratchy. On game days the big fear was always thunderstorms. Then I'd worry we'd be rained out—fretted about it from the moment I rolled out of bed—but that was one thing that never actually happened. Right now, though, it's damn cold—teeth-chattering cold—and I didn't bring clothes for this.

You never know about the weather this time of year in Indiana, or any other time of year. Freeze in the winter, swelter in the summer, and get blown away in the spring—these are the rules you learn to live by here. If you don't, you're out of luck.

And if you can't imagine someone being really worried about thunderstorms, you need to spend some time in the Midwest.

I feel like a madman, standing here with my teeth chattering as I strain to hear Dad on the loudspeaker again. I can hear the ballpark, but I'm still too far away to see it. Is this the only memory of him available to me? This hallucination of his voice? I can stand here and freeze, waiting to hear the voice of a ghost... or I can turn back. But why am I still waiting, as if unable to move—

"STEPPING UP TO THE PLATE, NUMBER 16, FREDDY BARNES.

BATTER UP!"

There he is—finally! Freddy Barnes.

I remember this moment—the first time Dad announced the Kokomo Rangers' towering left fielder. We were in the announcer's box during my first season, and it was the very first time we announced a game together, when everything was still so new to me. I'd heard Freddy's name before, but I'd never seen him—he was HUGE. Dad filled me in on his stats—batting average, runs, walks, RBIs, base on balls, strikeouts, and, scariest of all, homers. Eight balls blasted out of the park last year, and he looked like he'd hit even more homers this year—and he did, eleven in all, including one that supposedly landed right here on Market Street where I'm standing now, freezing my face off.

"How do you know this stuff?" I asked Dad. Freddy settled into his stance at the plate. I was truly puzzled.

"Word gets around," Dad said quietly.

I hoped I'd see one of Freddy's tape-measure home runs, and just then he cranked a ball to deep center field. Dad and I both stood up. For a second, it looked like it was hit hard enough to clear the fence, but the center fielder jumped up against the fence and snagged the drive just before it left the park—

"FLYOUT TO CENTER FIELD!"

There's Dad again—his voice booming through the loudspeaker—across the field and the stands, making the call like *he* was the umpire and running the game. After the call, we would've recorded the play: a flyout to center field, marked F-8 in the scorecard no matter who hit the ball or caught it.

The Announcers

That outcome was never marked any other way—it'd never change, nor would any of the symbols Dad taught me. Each and every symbol always represented the same thing. Nothing could ever happen on the field that those symbols didn't explain. There were no variations, and there still aren't—nothing that happens on the ball field today can be recorded any differently than it was back then, including when Freddy Barnes flew out to deep center field.

But there are no symbols in baseball for death—so how can I score your death, Dad?

You taught me how to keep score in a game, but what I needed was lessons on keeping score in real life. I'm still trying to sort that out. Oddly, even though there's no scorekeeping symbol for death, after that moment in the movie theatre—that Thursday afternoon when Grandma came looking for me, searching among the rows, bearing the awful news—after that moment, every scorekeeping symbol I'd learned became associated with death.

"COMING UP TO THE PLATE, NUMBER 6, THE RIGHT FIELDER, JACK LEWIS."

Dad's announcing *me* at bat now. His voice sounds the same as it did before—yet I'm feeling... more and more... like it's further away.

I walk closer to the field to hear better. Number 6—the right fielder—yes, that was me after I got used to the Nationals being the worst team in the league. How did Dad refer to our sorry lot? Oh, yeah. "You're maybe one or two players short," he said, "and a long shot to win the league."

Fortunately he didn't stop there, and Dad went on to say I had a chance to break into the lineup early. All I had to do was work hard and prove myself. If I proved myself, I'd be playing in every Nationals game. And deep down, I knew this would make Dad proud, to see me out there every time he was up in the announcer's box, even though I didn't truly understand why I felt this way.

Yet while Dad was painting such a rosy picture of my future baseball prospects, I was still far from convinced. He must've been reading my mind because he told me look out on the field. "Go out there and see how it feels," he said. "Take a long, hard look. It appears they've mowed the grass especially for you."

The grass was very green and plush, I thought, but mowed and manicured like any field would be. "Take it gradual like," Dad called. "It won't take too long for you to get your feet on the ground."

I was in awe. "It won't?" My voice was almost a whisper.

Dad looked me square in the eyes. His voice was barely louder than mine. "Not at all. And don't forget. Lefties generally don't play shortstop, or second or third base, so don't waste your time with those positions. Catchers always have to worry about foul tips and getting creamed by the runner coming in from third, so skip that one too." He paused for a second, hesitating. "Also, in case you need remindin', watch the outfield fences."

I don't know if it was the expression on his face or the way he said it, but there was something in Dad's words that went well beyond baseball.

The Announcers

"NUMBER 6 IS ENTERING THE FIELD FOR THE FIRST TIME AS A STARTER. LET'S GIVE HIM A WARM WELCOME!"

Dad's voice from the past is getting me lost in the present. In my mind, I can see myself walking onto the field—that first time when he told me to get a feel for it, when I heard him announce, my first time in the starting lineup. If I had any sense, I'd turn around and tend to the business that brought me to Kokomo in the first place by going straight to the funeral home.

But...

But I hate viewings and funerals.

I stood above Dad's coffin, smelling the sickly sweet flowers, and didn't cry. Not once. To this day I've worn the pain of that moment like a badge of honor.

So even though I'm standing here, freezing in the street instead of attending Uncle Mike's funeral, and hearing a voice from forty years in the past—maybe I really am where I'm supposed to be.

In a way, I'm attending a different kind of memorial. Very different. And very important. And, no matter how painful, it's the first memorial in my life I've wanted to attend.

Chapter 12

Finding my true position in right field that first year and breaking into the starting lineup was a big deal. Those accomplishments gave Dad something to enjoy in his remaining time—something I fully realized one day when the two of us were on our way to Northside. "We're headed back out there," Dad said cheerfully. I looked over at him, and the expression on his face matched the tone of his voice exactly. I told myself I'd never forget the scene, and I haven't.

Remaining time...

Even now, saying that phrase makes me uneasy. Anything that reminds me of that time—the time between when Dad came back from Mayo Clinic and when he'd leave us forever—makes me uneasy.

Maybe part of that feeling has to do with us—Ann and me—being kept in the dark about Dad's condition. As far as we knew, there was no "condition"—even though I could feel something looming over all our lives like a great black cloud of silence. And I didn't know it at the time, but that cloud started to appear around us as soon as Dad got off the train. There was so much in plain sight—so many clues and cues and moments in plain sight—that I should've noticed. The writing was on the wall, but I didn't have the guts to make it out. And there are no second chances...

But—to escape for a moment from those torturous thoughts—during that first year of Little League, I found a new chance to impress Dad. It turned out that I could gun down runners at home plate all the way from my spot in right field. It wasn't a complete surprise, given how the coach commented so much on my strong throwing arm during tryouts, but Dad reacted as though it was—and that made throwing a runner out at home plate all the more special. Dad patted me on the back after the first time I managed to do it, and I could see the pride in his eyes. Come to think of it, that was only time I really could see pride in his eyes.

To tell the truth, I usually tried to avoid Dad's eyes. For a while it was because of what I found there—his innermost thoughts staring back at me with emotions I couldn't begin to understand. Later on, when his skin was yellow from jaundice, just looking at Dad was tough enough, let alone dare a glimpse into his tinged eyes.

As I looked down at the dirt, Dad regaled me with tales of how he did the same thing "once or twice in the good ol' days," back when he had a good arm and strong legs. This was one of the few times his voice sounded excited—like his memories had transported him back, and the journey made him into a new person.

Those days were clearly long gone, but what I would have given to be with him back then! To stand there on the field and take it all in, chatting with Dad as I'd watch him gun down runners at home and hit doubles and steal bases—watch Dad perform like a real-life baseball player, and a good one at that. I still feel this way; I always have.

But… Dad's voice didn't sound excited for very long… and I don't want to think about this now. I don't want to get stuck in another morass of bad memories… out here, in the freezing wind… but it's difficult to leave it alone… It's difficult to keep any of my thoughts free from the taint of that black cloud… free from the nothingness…

Dad's voice...

I can still hear how it sounded... not after that time on the field, when I first threw a runner out at home... but how it sounded when I overheard him arguing with Mom. It wasn't the first time I'd heard them argue—far from it—but it was one of the first times when I felt like I was listening to something I really shouldn't have heard.

My parents spent most of their time arguing, or at least it seemed this way to me, and I tried my best to ignore what they were saying, but this time I just couldn't—there was something about the sting of their words that was so... unusual, so different from normal. This was the start of something else—the start of arguments that would get worse as Dad got sicker. They must have argued hundreds of times, and though I've mostly forgotten what they fought about, I remember this time—this time, and one other time that was much, much worse.

These are some of my least favorite memories, and the first one begins with something bloody: a big slab of meat.

How typically Midwestern.

Sirloin was the cause of Mom and Dad's first big argument. We had it for supper at least three times a week because Dad's doctor said it would be good for him. Judging from all the commotion it caused, though, I don't think it did much good.

Mom and Dad would argue about sirloin all the time because sirloin for supper got very old very fast, despite Mom's attempts to serve it as many different ways as possible. Dad grew to hate sirloin—as we all did eventually—and said so whenever it was on the menu.

My parents' arguments on sirloin didn't vary much, and

they were quite predictable after the first time. They always went through the same steps: Mom brought up the topic, Dad reacted negatively, and then Mom tried to appease Dad. Pure and simple A to B to C, yet as time went by, Mom's attempts to appease Dad became more desperate—and angry.

In the beginning, though, Mom's voice was gentle and cajoling as she told Dad the menu for the evening. "We're having a big, juicy sirloin tonight," she'd say softly. To this day I never think of sirloin without this description—big and juicy—coming to mind in an almost whispery voice. I've never seen a sirloin that looked as good as Mom made them sound. And on a regular basis, Mom's steaks were "on special at Kroger's," which she said in attempt to make them sound more economical. Kroger's would have gone out of business if they had specials every time Mom said this.

After the first month of steak, Dad's response became less amused and more irritated. "Ugh! Steak again," he'd say, often adding "Do I have a choice?" in a raised voice. Dad had no idea how many times he raised his voice without being aware that he was doing it. And the more often he did it, the more I knew how much he hated this one cut of beef. After so many nights of this, I began to feel deeply sorry for Mom for having to concoct polite responses to Dad's attitude.

But somehow she managed to do this without fail. In many ways, listening to Mom grovel like this was the most difficult thing for me to sit through back then—and it's even harder for me now, now that I fully understand these scenes.

Mom's responses were a verbal barometer of sorts. The angrier and more desperate her voice became, the more that a storm was about to hit. These outbursts were intense—so

The Announcers

stormy that no one else could ever appreciate the mayhem it would wreak upon us unless they experienced it firsthand.

Recalling these episodes is something I try to avoid—the way Mom's voice, despite everything she knew about the situation, sounded so appealing when she described sirloin; the way Dad could never be convinced to enjoy sirloin again; the way their voices rose so high, I was afraid one of them would storm out of the house. No one ever did, but once… after Dad's illness began to accelerate… Mom mentioned sirloin for dinner, and Dad yelled, "DO I HAVE A CHOICE?"

And then came Mom's meek reply: "Do any of us?"

It was a watershed moment, and afterwards came a heaviness with a presence like a war monument—massive, quiet, and carved in stone to commemorate a moment when civility fell apart. No one walked out of the house, and no blood was shed, but something was different in their voices after that—something was broken.

But that moment seems like a mere pebble next to the other big argument I remember. A pebble, a grain of sand, a mote of dust—

This was worse than anything else that happened before Dad's death—even worse than Murgy, that goddamn bag of shit, though he did play a part in it—and thinking about it now leads me to a kind of no man's land of conversation. It's something I've tried to avoid thinking about for as long as I can remember, a detail that I'd give anything to forget about, something I wish never would've intruded upon my life and Ann's life, too, even though we've never discussed it—

During the surgery that made Murgy a permanent part of Dad's existence, the doctors had to sever some critical nerves once and for all. There was nothing they could do to avoid cutting these nerves; the surgery wouldn't have been possible otherwise. But these nerves were instrumental to maintaining Dad's manhood, instrumental to enabling him to make love to Mom. The doctors didn't call it impotence then. They were too indirect for language like that.

The first inkling I had of the problem came one night when I was falling asleep. My parents' bedroom was on the other side of the house from mine, and even though Mom's voice was barely a whisper, I could hear it. "What's wrong?" she said. She paused between her words, but if Dad was talking, I couldn't hear him. "I'm sorry, too," she continued. "We'll try another time… Maybe it will be only for a brief spell." She was trying to be nice to Dad, and she spoke to him with the same comforting tone she used when one of us was sick.

Dad mumbled something that I couldn't make out, but then came more of Mom's strange whispering. Somehow, it sounded like it was directed solely at me. "Something might be wrong," she said. "We'd better check." In hindsight, Mom's voice gave way from comforting to distant here, as though checking with the doctors was an afterthought.

The weird quality of Mom's voice—the way it seemed to seek me out—made me feel like she was telling me something that I should know. But I didn't have a clue as to what might be going on, though I had a strong feeling that it wasn't good. I wished it could stay that way, I wished I'd never learn what was happening, but I knew whatever it was couldn't stay secret for long.

No doubt Mayo Clinic took their call in a jiffy and politely reminded them of what they'd been told before: "An unfortunate side effect of the surgical procedure." I never heard whether those were the actual words, but I can imagine a doctor speaking them to Mom over the phone, using the softest tone he could manage. But what was or was not said didn't really matter, because whatever it was amounted to little more than a well-rehearsed euphemism, one taken from a shelf in a vast warehouse of sayings. Even then, it still had to come across as quite a shock to Mom and Dad—but their endurance still had yet to receive the hardest test.

There was more to come from the doctors—the parting gift that would tie everything up with a nice bow and send off my parents with a neatly wrapped package that could never be opened. Again, I don't entirely know what they were told next, but I can imagine it, imagine the doctor's considered opinion: "The 'effect' will be with you for quite a while."

For quite a while... or, in Dad's case, for the rest of his life.

Despite what they'd been told, Mom and Dad didn't give up trying to make love. During the next incident, I overheard Mom saying, "Don't think about it—just relax," and this time, her voice was much louder than a whisper. Dad was quiet, and so I had to wonder what was happening between them. I was still wondering until a week or so later, when I overheard Mom again. "I'm a bundle of nerves!" she said. "I *have* to go to the living room."

Have to—

HAVE TO—

Mom's voice is hammering in my ears like a pneumatic drill—

And then she *did* go to the living room. She walked right

past my bedroom, dragging her mattress and bedding behind her, and as she went, I felt some indefinable guilt creep over me, as though bearing witness made me feel guilty—as though overhearing and seeing their struggles somehow made them my fault. I couldn't believe it then, watching her walk past, and I still couldn't believe it when it happened for the second time, the eighth time, the fifty-fifth time—I lost count of them all... before I could lose my sense of disbelief... All those times I had to bear witness to something I didn't understand... the brutal truth behind Mom's compulsion to walk away from their bed—the schisms, the repercussions of Dad's impotence... their pretense that Dad wasn't dying... pretending for our benefit! And Mom dragging her mattress out into the living room and leaving Dad alone! Like there was something he should have done about the goddamn situation—like there was something any of us could have done! But there was nothing.

Night after night, she left him.

I pretended not to notice, and I never said a word.

Chapter 13

Tate Street looms ahead. When the spirit moves me, I'll mosey onward, and make the familiar turn to the left. Then I'll be approaching the park. It'll be on my left, exactly as it was when Dad drove me there so many years ago. The Taurus is behind me somewhere, but I don't feel much like turning around to confirm the fact. Funny, but now that I'm away from the car, I'm beginning to feel isolated—especially since the eleven-year-old me has disappeared again, taking my old bicycle and glove with him. I wonder if he'll reappear. There's no telling what he'll bring with him, especially since what I knew back then has been mashed up with the little tidbits and details Mom's revealed to me throughout the years—tidbits from the universe of facts hidden from Ann and me. But none of these facts were known to my eleven-year-old self, so maybe if he does reappear, he'll bring memories worth savoring with him.

I think I can hear something playing over the ballpark's loudspeaker—

"Take me out to the ball game…"

Ah, it's "Take Me Out to the Ball Game." Dad played it every time we went up to the booth. Whoever composed that little ditty did themselves proud. Each and every time he announced a game, the very first thing Dad did was put on that song.

I wish I had a buck for every time the lyrics of that song have gone through my head. There doesn't appear to be any rhyme or reason for why it pops into my head when it does.

Sometimes it's in the middle of a serious meeting, and I've had to cover up for those lapses more than a few times. Whenever it comes to mind, I'm taken back to the ballpark—sitting next to Dad in the scorekeeper's booth, standing out in right field, or staring out at the pitcher after digging my cleats into the dirt in the batter's box.

He wouldn't turn the volume up *all* the way, but it was pretty close. If the wind was blowing right, I wouldn't be surprised if folks five or six blocks away could hear it.

If I were playing that day, I'd run out to my position in right field while the song played on. This wasn't until I broke into the starting lineup, though, which was about a third of the way through that first season—and, no surprise, I broke into the lineup because of my bat. "Can't keep a good man on the bench," Dad said. He was smiling one of his rare smiles as he spoke to me. I seldom saw his face this way.

But Dad had reason to smile. I rarely struck out, and I had the habit of getting hits with runners on base. Dad said I was the opposite of Casey. I didn't understand what he meant, and he explained the story of "Casey at the Bat" to me, where Mighty Casey struck out when the game was on the line. *How could he have done that?* I wondered. I couldn't understand how someone couldn't deliver when the game was on the line, but I kept my mouth shut, and Dad kept talking. It seemed like he was a fountain of wisdom.

"Have at it," he advised. "Far better to go down swingin' with runners in scoring position than take a called third strike. Nothin' good ever happens when you get stuck standin' in the batter's box with the bat on your shoulder. And walks aren't good enough, either."

Dad wasn't smiling this time. Instead, the longer he talked, the more I could see he was trying to get something out of his eye. It took me a long time to figure out that he was trying to hide his tears. Later, Mom said Dad did a lot of crying whenever Ann and I were elsewhere.

But even with him hiding his tears, this particular conversation was the most I heard Dad talk. I'm sure there was considerably more on his mind that he never expressed—bundles and bundles worth—but words were always hard for him to come by. Even as young as I was, I picked up on this problem, so it makes this experience that much more remarkable. He talked to me more on this day than on any of the other days of my life.

I can still hear "Take Me Out to the Ball Game" over the loudspeaker. Judging by how far the sound is projecting, the old sound system must be in really good shape, even after all these years. I think this bodes well for the rest of the park—it should still be in tiptop shape, too.

Mom and Ann would be sitting in the stands. Mom's brother Norman and her parents would often be there too; it was definitely a family affair, each and every time, and I was the family star! But the most important thing about those days was that Dad invariably felt the best he ever did whenever he was at Northside. Murgy's antics, the assorted aches and pains that went along with having terminal cancer—all these things seemed to take a break when Dad was up in that booth.

By the time the season was over, the Nationals were a disaster, finishing in distant last—including a 26–0 thrashing at the hands of the Rangers. From a team standpoint, my first season wasn't a resounding success. But I broke into the starting lineup in right field, learned to hit—particularly with runners on base—and developed quite a reputation for throwing runners out at the plate… Unfortunately, I was also the slowest player on the team—if not the league.

Maybe if we'd stayed at the ballpark all the time, things would've worked out better than they did whenever we were anyplace else. Of course, that was impossible, and we left Northside as soon as each game was finished, stopping over at A&W for hot dogs and root beer on the way home. That postgame ritual happened just like clockwork—except this clock was running on superfast time. My first year of Little League ran away from us in a great big hurry—"faster than a speeding bullet," as the announcer used to proclaim on *Superman*—and all I could do was go along for the ride holding on as best I could.

Some days were better than others, with one important qualifier. "Better" never meant "easy." Each time the hands of the clock made a complete revolution, new signs that all was not well crept into our family dynamic—

Signs that our family was falling apart.

These signs were everywhere, and it became all the more difficult for me to overlook them as time went on. Despite the diversion provided by Little League, our family—and Dad specifically—was on a downhill course, and there wasn't one thing we could have done to change it—not when the clock was ticking away like a time bomb.

I can only speculate, but Dad not being able to tell us about his condition must have made it almost impossible to keep going. But keep going he did, working two jobs until almost his last day.

The Announcers

Too bad there's not a hall of fame for this. He would've been a shoe-in.

But even if Mom and Dad had us fooled, Dad couldn't hide his troubles from Mom. She told me all about it much later. I don't remember exactly when she told me, but I hadn't been married long, so it must've been around '68 or '69. The story itself, however, took place in 1956, about five weeks before the start of my second season of Little League. Dad was trying his very best to conceal how bad he felt even from her. But she could read him like a book, so finally she laid it on the line and told Dad that he had to go see the doctor in Indianapolis.

All Dad did in response was agree. No one in Kokomo was equipped to handle how sick he was. They worked it out so Ann and I were at school when they went. We didn't even know they were gone.

The doctor who saw Dad was named Dr. Hardy. He was an oncologist, and Mayo Clinic had sent him all of Dad's records. Mom kept an invoice from Dr. Hardy's office as a souvenir—she was holding it in her hand when she told me this story. I cringed when I saw it then, and I'm cringing as I think about it now.

Mom and Dad had to travel through a fairly wicked thunderstorm on the way down to Indianapolis. "It was a preview of things to come," she said, looking at me to gauge my reaction. I bowed my head. "Sure was," I said. I never kept track, but it always seemed like bad weather got in the way of driving to and from Indianapolis. During this trip, Mom drove while Dad mostly slept. This arrangement caused some trouble once they reached the hospital.

"Your father awoke with a start," Mom said, "and he thought he was back at Mayo Clinic." Then she paused. I could see it was difficult for her to continue. Finally, she spoke again, haltingly. "He should have... known... it wasn't... because... there wasn't... any snow... on the ground. But... it... might as well... have been... for what we were about to go through."

"I'm sorry," I mumbled.

"Tommy's on pins and needles..." she said, seeming to see Dad as though he was there with us—and suddenly I knew she'd fallen back into her memories. She spoke as though I wasn't even in the room. "I thought we'd be kept waiting for an hour or two, but the nurse is telling us to go right in. 'The doctor will be here momentarily,' she's saying. I didn't catch her name," Mom said, choking back her tears, "but I'd rather wait than listen to what I'm about to hear. Wait until the cows come home... but that's not going to happen..."

I wished Mom would stop right then and there because I knew where all this was headed, but she wasn't about to. Her brain was running through these horrific memories like a runaway car barreling through a crowded street.

"We're both sitting down," she continued, "and I'm fidgeting in my seat. I don't have a clue as what to do with my hands. Suddenly they're on my lap and I'm staring down at them and in less than a minute, *he's here*—Dr. Hardy, I mean. He's carrying papers on a clipboard EXACTLY like Dr. Winslow at Mayo's did. Maybe they're the same papers, but there's no way of knowing that without asking him and I'm not about to do that.

"Suddenly, before Dr. Hardy can say anything, Tommy blurts out, 'They told me a while back that there could be three years in the cards, doc! Sometimes I feel I won't make it through the next three days—and this is one of those times.'"

How could Dad ever do that? I wondered. *How could he just give up?* But Mom didn't give me any time to think.

"Oh, God," she said, still reliving the memory. "I just want to run away and hide. Dr. Hardy's taken aback by Tommy's outburst. Taken aback and confused. He's asking how long ago Tommy was told that. I should know this off the top of my head but I can't remember... *I can't...* So... so... I'm rummaging through my purse to get my calendar. I know it'll be in there... I know it'll be in there!"

Mom and Dad both were wilting under the pressure, but Dr. Hardy seemed to come to Mom's rescue: he checked the records and determined Dad had been told he had three years to live a mere year and a half before. As Mom recalled, neither she nor Dad mentioned to Dr. Hardy how they'd kept Dad's illness a secret from my sister and me. I wonder if that information would've changed the doctor's calculations—the unavoidable task of recalculating Dad's remaining time—because it seemed to affect what happened next while they all mentally did the math.

Normally, Dad was a true genius at arithmetic, and he could crunch numbers as rapidly as a calculator—maybe quicker—and since the cancer hadn't invaded his brain, he should've been able to come up with an estimate right away. But, as the seconds ticked past, something was clearly wrong. Dad's brain was balking—he couldn't come up with the answer—and this new development unnerved him and Mom both.

Dr. Hardy attempted to compensate for the lull in conversation by engaging in small talk—stupid, incessant, small talk. Small talk about a blizzard in Indianapolis when Mom and Dad were at Mayo's, about how his snow tires really got a workout, about how those very same snow tires had to be replaced every three years—

Painted into a corner by his own words, Dr. Hardy glanced up from his charts and looked at Mom. Mentioning that there was a note in Dad's chart, he commented on how sick she'd been at the time—borderline if not full-blown pneumonia—and how she was extremely lucky not to have been admitted. Mom said nothing, and an uncomfortable silence ensued as Dr. Hardy tapped his papers. Mom was certain Dr. Hardy would tell them what they were anxiously waiting to hear, but instead the doctor rambled onward, expressing his sorrow that Mom and Dad hadn't made it home for Christmas when they were at Mayo's, throwing in another mention of his snow tires and the weather and driving and cars until Dad finally lost it. "AND HOW MANY MONTHS DO I HAVE TO GO, DOCTOR?" he yelled.

Clearly flustered, Dr. Hardy took a pen from his pocket and started writing calculations. He became so engrossed in the task, he erroneously referred to the clipboard as the "scorecard."

"The scorecard," he said. "Thank God for scorecards! A few quick calculations, and I'll have the answer for you in a second. It's absolutely essential to maintain a handle on the scorekeeping." Baseball—he'd lapsed into baseball jargon while Dad's life was on the line!

Dr. Hardy finished his calculations but, instead of immediately revealing his answer, he told Dad to get up on the table so he could examine him. After telling Dad to unbutton his shirt and lie down on his back, Dr. Hardy turned to Mom. "When did his face begin to turn yellow?" he asked.

Mom hemmed and hawed, coughing. "A... few months... and... no more," she said finally. "It simply can't be any longer than that."

This was tough for them—very tough. Something they'd feared and refused to discuss with each other was out in the open. There it was! But instead they said nothing as Dr. Hardy continued his poking and prodding. When he finished, he repeated the examination. The absence of sound in the room became oppressive.

Dr. Hardy sighed and looked at Mom. A third examination wasn't necessary.

"I'm afraid I already know the answer," she said, "but how is he?"

"His liver's enlarged," Dr. Hardy said. "More than likely, there's involvement there, which is exactly what was predicted. Everything is running true to form."

"'True to form?' How exactly is that, doctor? What will happen next? Isn't there something you can give him?"

"There's nothing to be done."

"And? How about the three years?"

"Maybe a fifty-fifty chance that he'll have all of them." He paused. "If things go well."

There it was—if things go well.

A goddamn coin toss.

Mom couldn't tell me more than that. She began crying softly and couldn't stop. But there was no need. I had heard enough—her story was the slightest flame illuminating what my eleven-year-old eyes hadn't been able to see.

As Mom and Dad left Dr. Hardy's office, the second season of Little League was still set to go, but now it was firmly held within fate's fickle clutches—and every coming day was tinged by the coin toss, by the crapshoot of events we'd yet to live, by Dad's increasingly yellow skin. One consequence of the cancer's extensive lymph-node involvement—jaundice—had come to pass, and it had occurred in the time frame originally projected. Dad's dying was going according to schedule.

Chapter 14

The wind and snow have stopped, but the temperature's still uncomfortably chilly. The sky is a discouraging gray, extending downward to envelope everything at eye level. I'm a block from the ballpark now, but I still can't see it. If it weren't such a strong place in my memories, I wouldn't have a clue as to where I am. The weather feels like Minnesota, but the city itself is a ghost town—run-down houses, bare trees, islands of sparse grass, and junked cars parked in yards. It looks like someone fought and lost a war here. And to think I chose to come back.

This trip is testing me in ways I hadn't imagined, and I haven't even reached my destination. What's actually waiting for me there? I'm not eager to find out, but turning back is out of the question. Dad's voice is pulling me onward. I don't understand why any of this is happening, whether I'm hallucinating and losing my mind, but there's no other way for it to be—and maybe that's all right. The city's so different now, it'd be easy for me to get lost—lost here, in my childhood hometown—if it wasn't for Dad's voice calling to me like a beacon from the past.

Come to think of it, there were times when I heard Dad's voice crack as he announced my name and number. I couldn't get a good glimpse of him because he was up in the announcer's box. *I'll ask him about this later,* I'd think, and filed the thought away in the back of my mind. The one time I actually did ask him was more than enough—Dad got the strangest expression on his face and quickly changed the subject.

I'm closer to the park now, but his voice doesn't seem to be any louder. Maybe it's the wind. If I have a truly special memory of Dad in me, it should be coming to me soon, since I'm getting so close to the source. We spent so much time together here.

But now, somehow, it feels like I'm getting further and further away even when I stand still. The wind is picking up, shoving me all over the street—

Something's—I can hear something coming through the air—

> "HOW COULD YOU NOT CRY
> WHEN THEY BURIED ME?"

It's... it's Dad... but his voice is warped... and he never announced this. Not over the loudspeaker, not in life. I asked myself this, and I wrote these words, wrote them over and over. So many times... over so many years... because... because this is the source of my pain.

The wind is frigid, cutting, tossing me around, but it's not the wind pulling me into the vortex of the past. It's memories... memories I hate...

they're letting me walk up to dad's coffin alone the carpet is

squishy-soft it's scary quiet

i have to do this like i was told be strong for mom and not cry not cry when the inside of my face feels like it's going to explode swirling like a whirlwind and I'm caught in an invisible trap i can't move but i i don't want to either don't want to be a nuisance don't

The Announcers

   want to make noise   dad's below me   in his box   and not making any noise either   it shouldn't be this way   but it it doesn't matter

     dad's beneath me   all i have to do is lower my head   and i'll be able to see him   say goodbye to him   this time before they   take him away   say goodbye   this time because i wasn't able to before   before   when he didn't come home

   from the hospital   and i didn't go   even though he asked

    to see me   i know i won't   have another chance   to say goodbye

      no one's told me this   but i know it anyway   they'll carry dad out   to the cemetery   before i can   say anything maybe i can practice   saying goodbye first

   "g-g— goodbye d-d-dad…"

   but nothing   coming from dad   no response nothing no one   told me about this   about how hard it would be   no one's told me much   of anything except mom's my   responsibility now

    one   last   goodbye before i watch them   close the lid and carry him out to be buried   in that hole   they dug for him   i'll be out there for that too   sitting under a canopy   and watching   except the lid will be closed   over dad

    it's like   all the steps   are written down   in my mind and all i   have to do   is set the thing in motion

     me—

    it makes me feel better   thinking of it this way   like a

J. G. Perkins

domino's about to be knocked down   in front   of a row of dominos   eventually all of them will be down

   until   someone puts them back up if they ever do

   dad's domino   has been   knocked down forever

   i'm hoping someone picks me back up   but i guess i guess   i'll have to wait   and see   if that happens

   my head   feels like   it's   being pushed down   but i'm trying   to keep it up

   dad was never much good   at goodbyes   he's called me a chip off   the old block   and i can't say that   i'm not much good   at goodbyes   either

   but then what does   the chip do   when the block's nowhere to be found

   i'm hot and sweaty   it's stuffy in here   i can smell all the flowers   and they're making me sick

   my   mind is   trying   to go somewhere else   to escape but it's   stuck here   these flowers are so awful   i'll never be able

   to go into a flower shop again   without   thinking of death

   my eyes are opening   all by themselves now   opening and looking down

   at dad   his face is pointed   up at me   like he's looking at me   but his eyes   are closed   dad's eyes are closed   and he   doesn't want to see me   no, it's not that—

   dad can't see me   because   he's not   not alive

The Announcers

NO

   i don't want to say this   can't say   it
but   i have to   but i want dad   to be smiling up at me
more than anything   in the world   smiling and   telling
me   none of this is really happening!

   i'm such an idiot   expecting dad to smile   up at me
as if   he's about to

   say hello   but dad   is not

   what is it i'm   trying   to say

   HE'S DEAD

   there   i've said   it

   something's   different   in dad's face   it doesn't seem
like   he's smiling

   his face looks peaceful   if only he   wasn't dead   not in
pain   not yellow not angry

   but dead   DEAD   unalive   unloving

   i want to look away   but can't   want to cry   but can't
want to run away

   but can't

   all there is   for me   is   dad's death

   and the person beneath me   who was dad   is no longer
a person

   no dad   no longer   with me   no   longer
with   me

   the person who was dad   is gone   he's   already left me
floating

   like a bubble   further and further away   never to

J. G. Perkins

return

   NO!

     i want to   reach out for him   one last time
but i can't

     somehow i've got to   get to a different place   got to get to
another

     memory   another feeling time place moment   anything else
but this

     anything   but this—

From that moment on, I've been nowhere else… I've been here, alone in this vortex. Every success, every joy, every moment of love comes back to this—everything is kept at a distance—everything is swallowed up by the void created by the one unanswerable question…

"How could you not cry when they buried me?"

Chapter 15

I'm a few blocks away from the ballpark, but something strange has caught my eye.

Up ahead on my right is a row of houses. All of them seem to be blurry except one. The grayness that's settled in everywhere around me doesn't seem to cover this house. At first I didn't think there was anything unusual about this house—it's rundown like all the rest around here, barely able to stay standing—but then I noticed something in the front yard. Next to an old Dodge on cinderblocks lay a pile of junk. Again, nothing out of the ordinary, but as I looked closer, I saw something unmistakable: a dining room table exactly the same as the one we had in the house on Mulberry Street. It was warped and splintered in places, but I recognized the design in the table's surface—and the memories started flooding in.

That table and its chairs took up a good part of our kitchen, but all four of us were somehow able to squeeze in. Ann sat at the end of the table closest to the stove, with Mom on her right and me on Mom's right. All of us sat opposite of Dad, who sat by himself directly across from me. There was a crack in the ceiling above him that we joked came from Dad blowing his top, which he did regularly during supper. It wasn't the kind of joke that made us laugh, though, and especially not during this supper. This particular supper wasn't just any supper—it's one that's stuck in my mind more than all the rest throughout the years—the absolute worst we shared together. It occurred two weeks before the start of the second season of Little League, and given everything that happened, it would've been a smart move to treat that supper like a ballgame and call everything off due to stormy weather...

The night's menu featured sirloin, mashed potatoes, green beans, and apple pie. I can almost see Dad shaking his head in disgust at the sight of those steaks. Though I didn't really notice it then, Dad was moving more slowly, hesitating before each task as though he'd rather sleep than deal with whatever came next. As the rest of us entered the kitchen, we didn't notice Dad—we were too busy looking at Mom. She was crying and trying to hide her tears.

"Is something wrong?" Ann asked.

Mom shook her head violently. "No!"

Ann was startled. Her lip started to tremble.

"No," Mom said, calmer. "It's nothing for you to fret yourselves about, kids. I just have something in my eye." Later, I learned that right before serving dinner, Mom had to clean up another of Dad's giant messes in the bathroom, shit and all.

Dad must've simply sat there in his chair and watched us as we entered. We followed Mom past the table over to the stove, still not noticing him.

"Are you *sure* you're all right?" I asked Mom, wanting to help her in any way possible.

I could tell this question made her mad. "I'm absolutely positive," she said, practically stamping her foot. "For the second time, I HAVE SOMETHING IN MY EYE! How many times do I have to explain something to you?" Her voice was much sharper than intended.

Ann kept her eyes glued on Mom. "Where's Dad?" she almost shouted. It as if we were all afraid to look where he was sitting—afraid of what we'd see instead.

"He's right where he should be," Mom mumbled, her eyes migrating over to Dad.

"Is everything okay?" I interjected stupidly, my voice tinged with desperation.

"I told you that it was okay the first time," she said, her voice harsh at first. She looked at me and saw I was struggling. "Yes," she said, more gently, "yes, everything's fine. I think I got a 'good do' on one of your favorites—the mashed potatoes!"

"I love mashed potatoes!" I shouted, momentarily distracted.

"And gravy," Ann added. "Don't forget the gravy!" She couldn't stand to be outdone.

"Don't worry, I won't," Mom reassured us—as if mashed potatoes could solve all our problems.

Finally, Dad stirred, clearing his throat slightly. "DAD!" Ann erupted. I turned and saw him looking up at Ann, smiling feebly. Both of us scampered over toward him but stopped short, hesitating, and moved to our chairs instead. Mom walked over to the table as Dad rose to stand with us.

Why didn't I notice Dad before? I thought. *How could we have missed him?*

"Hi kids," Dad said. His voice was so soft we could barely hear him. He glanced over at Mom, perhaps trying to read how she'd reacted to his latest mess in the bathroom, but Mom avoided his gaze.

"I might have burnt the meat a tad," she said apologetically.

All of us focused on the center of the table, where the steaks were neatly piled on a plate.

"I know," Dad mumbled, halfheartedly trying to conceal his contempt for sirloin. As he spoke, Dad swayed slightly but steadied himself against the chair.

Mom's eyes widened, but she chose to ignore Dad's unsteadiness. "You always want it well-done anyway," she said, her hands on her hips. "I cooked an extra one in case you want it. Sirloin will do you good."

It was the same old line Mom had used a thousand times, but Ann and I didn't understand why it was so tiresome to Dad. He rolled his eyes.

"I'm hungry!" Ann exclaimed.

"We're having steak *again?*" I asked.

"Oh, come on," Mom said, looking directly at me. "I bet none of your friends get to have steak half as often as you do." She tried to make her words sound funny, but none of us laughed.

Dad was staring straight at the pile of steaks, his face almost grim. "Not that well-done I bet, but this will be just fine," he said. Something in Dad's voice told me he was lying. I noticed him swaying again and looked over at Mom—her face was aghast. Dad nearly fell on the floor and she rushed toward him, somehow masking her movements and making them look casual.

"You've caught your trousers on the edge of the table," she said to Dad. "Here, let me get them." She bent over, pretending to free Dad's trousers from the table, and helped him sit down. She moved back around the table, and then, finally, all of us took our seats.

None of us spoke. The seconds passed like years. "Is something wrong?" I asked Dad. I might as well have thrown a lit match into a pool of gasoline.

"Why must something always be wrong?" Dad said gruffly. "It doesn't have to be, you know!"

Mom struggled to our rescue. "There's a bug going around," she lied. She wasn't any better than Dad. "Don't know where I heard it," she continued, "but I did. Hope none of us catch it." Her face looked like it would break at any moment.

Dad looked down, feeling guilty for his outburst. "I know I don't have the flu," he said somberly.

"A bug?" Ann asked innocently.

"The flu, stupid!" I attacked.

"I'm not stupid," she said, looking from Mom to Dad. "He called me stupid!"

Mom looked at both of us, exasperated. "He didn't mean to—"

"Make him say he's sorry!" Ann demanded.

Dad put his covered his ears, trying to block everything out, but then clenched his fists. "KIDS, PLEASE DON'T ARGUE!" he exploded.

Ann and I were shaken. It wasn't the first time Dad lost control, but it was happening more and more frequently. As were Mom's excuses.

Mom stepped in before either of us could start crying.

"Let's start passing the food before it gets cold," she said as calmly as she could. She picked up the plate of steaks and handed it to Ann, who turned toward me and stuck out her tongue. Satisfied, she turned back toward Mom.

"Thanks," she said, and took the smallest steak for herself.

She started to pass the plate to Dad, but Mom intervened. "Let me have it," she said, her voice fatigued. Holding the plate firmly in hand, she looked at Dad as he chose a steak. "It would be easier if I held them for you, Tommy. That way you won't have to worry about passing the plate clear across the table." I looked over at Dad's hands, and they seemed to tremble ever so slightly.

I butted in like a bull in a china shop. "I could hold it for Dad! I'm closer."

"No way! You'd drop them for sure," Ann taunted.

"No I wouldn't."

"Yes you would!"

Mom grew impatient. "Leave it be!" she said. She turned calmly back to Dad like nothing had happened. "Besides, I'm already holding the steaks for your father. The biggest one's on top."

Dad gathered all his strength to match Mom's effort as he reached out and speared the biggest steak. "Anyone else want it?" he said, trying to keep the moment light. "Come on, no takers? Going once... going twice... well then, if there aren't any more bids, I guess it's mine—burnt to a crisp or otherwise."

For a moment, Dad's voice sounded completely alive, but

Mom wasn't fooled. She frowned. "I didn't say the steak was *that* well-done," she said.

Dad put the steak on his plate and gave it a quick examination. "No, matter of fact, you didn't. The meat looks more well-done than usual, but I'm sure it'll go down just fine," he said.

"My steak doesn't look burnt at all," Ann said. "How would it look if it was burnt to a crisp?"

All of a sudden, my stomach felt queasy. "I'm not very hungry," I said.

"The steaks are fine," Mom scolded. "And don't forget that they're good for us."

"For *almost* everything that ails us," Dad interjected. He started massaging his eyebrows with one hand, as though he'd suddenly become very weary. I don't know how I missed the sarcasm in his voice—or what he really meant—but I did.

"What do you mean by 'almost?'" Ann asked.

My queasiness increased. "Is something wrong?" I whined. "Is… is everything all right?" I felt like I was catching only ten percent of what was happening around the table.

Mom flashed angry glances at Ann and Dad before picking her steak. As she set it on her plate, her hands started to shake and she almost dropped her utensils onto the table. She pretended like nothing had happened as she addressed us. "Your father is trying to be funny," she said sternly, then put on a false cheerfulness. "Don't forget—I cooked one extra steak in case anyone wants it."

"We'll hold a lottery to see whoever might be the winner,"

Dad said. I could tell something was wrong with his voice.

"I don't want another steak," Ann said.

"Are you sure everything's all right?" I implored, attempting to stifle a cough. My asthma was starting to act up.

Mom patted me on the shoulder. "Yes, everything's fine," she said. "Now, how about some of those mashed potatoes you wanted so much?"

Ann grabbed Mom's arm. "And the gravy? I thought you made gravy."

"Don't worry," Mom reassured, "the gravy will come next. I made it from your favorite recipe."

"Goody!" Ann exclaimed.

"But first," Mom started, "here's the mashed po—"

Suddenly, Dad stood up from the table, gripping his right side. "I'll be right back," he moaned, and ran from the table. These were the same words that he'd say before he went to the hospital for the last time.

I stood up from the table to follow Dad, but Mom restrained me. "I WANT TO HELP HIM!" I pleaded, thrashing to get loose, but her grip was firm.

"Better that you stay here for now," she instructed me. "Your father will be right back."

"When?" Ann asked.

"Soon."

Mom still held me in her clutches. "Is he going to the bathroom again?" I asked. I hoped not, because bad things usually happened in the bathroom.

"I... I think so," Ann said. "Is he sick?"

"Remember the bug I mentioned?" Mom said hastily.

"The flu?" I said.

"Something like that."

"Will we catch it?" Ann asked.

"But Dad said he doesn't have it," I said.

"Do you mean... the three of us?" Mom said, taken aback slightly. "We won't catch it if we eat properly. Please remember this while our food gets colder as I flap my gums."

Temporarily distracted, Ann and I began to fill our plates when Dad suddenly re-entered the kitchen. He'd changed shirts. "False alarm from Murgy," he said. "Consider it another of his practical jokes—sending out signals for a red alert when nothin's about to happen."

Mom seemed to ignore Dad as she held the mashed potatoes for Ann. "They're just like I promised," she said. "Take some, and I'll hand them over to your brother."

As Mom passed the bowl to me, she said, "Load up!" Then she turned to Dad, who'd just begun to recline in his chair. "You're back," she said.

"HA HA HA!" Dad laughed, but there was nothing funny about what Mom said. I didn't know it then, but this was the most horrible laugh I'd ever hear.

Mom seemed stunned. Her mouth moved a couple times without saying anything. "Is everything... alright?" she said finally, seeming to parrot me.

"I hope you are able to see the humor in all this," Dad said.

"Just a little trickle of blood on my shirt and nothing more. Hardly worth a second thought, but I got me a fresh one anyway." To emphasize his point, Dad touched his shirt with both hands.

Repulsed by the mere mention of blood, Ann turned away from Dad. "Pass me the gravy," she said to Mom.

"It was my own dad-burned fault," Dad continued, "getting my shirt blood-stained like that—"

Mom cut him off like a guillotine. "We'll handle the gravy in the same way we did the mashed potatoes," she said.

Dad persisted. "I didn't seal Murgy properly, so there won't be a gold star for me today."

"Would you like some gravy on your mashed potatoes?" I asked Dad.

Mom saw that I was literally drowning my potatoes and lightly chided me, her voice

suddenly trailing off. A moment passed, and she seemed to shake herself awake. "Now for the green beans," she said, louder again but more tense, "and we can start shoveling in the grub."

Ann turned toward Dad. "Why do you have on a different shirt?" She seemed to be trying to stare right through him.

Where the hell have you been for the last ten minutes? I thought.

"Oh, well... it..." Dad sputtered. "It... was, so... I thought—"

"His other shirt was dirty," Mom explained angrily. "You could tell it a mile away."

"I couldn't—" Ann protested.

"Really dirty, dirty," Dad said to Ann.

"If we don't dig in now, our supper won't be fit to eat!" Mom said, and that put an end to the moment. We started eating, and the conversation lulled. After a long silence, Mom spoke up. "Not bad if I do say so myself," she observed.

Ann made a face at her plate. "I never liked green beans."

"Try to eat some anyway," Mom begged. "They're good for you."

"But I don't want to grow faster," Ann said.

"Can I put some gravy on your mashed potatoes?" I asked Dad for a second time.

"I have enough gravy," Dad snapped.

"Are you sure?"

"It's fine," Dad said, his voice rising. "Fine!"

"It wouldn't be any trouble."

"It's fine it's fine it's fine IT'S FINE! How many times do I have to tell you that it's fine?" he screamed.

I was trying not to listen, trying to shut everything out. "Calm down, dear," Mom said. "Please calm down. You're about to blow your top and make the crack in the ceiling worse." She smiled faintly. "No one wants that."

"Do you mean make the one I've already made there worse?" he corrected her, his voice boiling with sarcasm. It was the tone I heard him use more often than anything else.

I wanted to tell Dad I was sorry, but my chest started to tighten. "I— I—" I began before bursting into a coughing fit, then knocked over my milk glass.

Ann pointed at me. "He's made a big mess!" she shouted gleefully.

I couldn't stop coughing. "I— I'm— sor—"

Mom quickly rose from her seat. "We'll get that up in a jiffy," she said. Her eyes couldn't hide the turmoil within.

I wanted her reassurances to make me feel better, but they didn't. "Let me help," I offered between coughing spasms. I wanted to do *anything* I could to make up for the mess I made.

"No, stay in your seat," she said. "I've almost gotten it taken care of."

Trying to distract everyone, Mom turned to Dad and started talking about baseball. "The big game's in two weeks," she reminded him. "I'm sure you're looking forward to it." If only she'd ended with that. She turned her attention to me and added, "I really like your new uniform. I can't believe how time flies."

At "time flies," Dad's eyes lit up like twin beacons. He looked directly at Mom and cleared his throat. "Time's not flying," he said. "It's a scythe cutting down everything in front of it."

There was something about the tone of Dad's voice that scared us, and Mom must have picked up on it, too. "What… what in the world are you talking about?" she asked, bewildered.

"Like overgrown grass, with me standing in the middle," Dad replied.

"Y-yes," Mom said, flustered, "but why—why mention—"

"Because I can see the blade just outside the window," Dad interrupted.

I didn't know why, but I felt like I had to stop Mom and Dad real fast, no matter how stupid I sounded. "I like my new uniform better than the old one—a lot better," I said quickly.

My distraction kept Mom together. "I kinda grew attached to the old one," she said.

Ann looked out the window, as if trying to see the blade Dad mentioned. She was too young to understand that Dad wasn't talking about a real blade, so not finding anything just made her more frustrated. She turned her attention to me, a mischievous grin suddenly spreading across her face.

"Remember when *he* hit a baseball through our window?" she said, pointing at me.

"Shall we hold off on that subject until another day?" Mom asked.

But I could tell Dad was furious, if not confused trying to remember the event, and his anger overrode Mom's response. "How does this have anything to do with what I just said?"

But Ann was far from deterred. She pointed at me for emphasis. "*He* went outside to play in the side yard while we were sitting here and finishing our supper—" she said, reveling.

"I have a headache—" Mom said, trying to escape.

"—and *he* was batting the baseball right toward the house," Ann continued.

I felt as if she'd slapped me. "No! I wasn't hitting right at it!" I shouted.

"The ball landed right there!" Ann squealed, pointing to the middle of the table. "It splattered food all over us!"

"It's coming back to me," Dad muttered.

"I don't think we need to go into that now," Mom admonished.

"I didn't mean to," I pleaded, and another coughing fit overtook me.

Ann was winning. She recognized this and was old enough to know when to press her advantage and go for the jugular. "You yelled at him," she said to Dad. "Don't you remember?"

I slouched in my chair, trying to keep from coughing. "I helped clean up the mess. Part of the cost of the new window came out of my allowance," I said defensively.

"Oh, how could I forget?" Dad said.

Mom finally laid down the law. "What did I *just* say? Could we please change the topic?" she said, and her voice was so sharp, no one dared cross her. "I might as well start clearing the table."

Ann and I averted our eyes to the floor. Even Dad seemed ashamed.

"I even went to the trouble of making apple pie as a special treat," Mom said, her face almost serene. "With vanilla ice cream."

Diverted but not totally discouraged, Ann turned to gaze out the window that was shattered by my fly ball. The sun shone in, its beams bathing Dad's face. She followed the light's path, and when her eyes rested on his face, she saw things… differently. I could tell something strange was happening as she looked back and forth between the window and Dad's face, her mouth hanging open, until her voice tore forth in a screech—"Dad's face is yellow!"

Almost immediately, Dad attempted to hide his face behind his hands. I kept my head bowed, not wanting to confront the reality of Ann's observation.

"You've just seen your father's face in a strange light," Mom explained.

"It *wasn't* the sun," Ann said defiantly.

"A very glaring sun," Mom offered.

Ann persisted. "Look at his hands!"

Dad turned his face to avoid Ann's stare.

Mom refused to look at Dad. "The light's still not quite right," she said. "It's always too dark in here."

Ignoring Mom, Ann squinted at Dad. "I can't see anymore, but his hands were the same color as his face," she said.

Mom's voice sounded as if she was reading a fairy tale. "The light can play tricks. It happens all the time," she said. I wanted to believe her—I *still* want to believe her.

"Is he still yellow?" Ann asked.

"He can't be!" The words leapt from my mouth. Despite my fear, I looked at Dad to see for myself.

"Don't!" Mom pleaded.

I was trying to see Dad's face, which forced him to turn his head back toward Ann. "See!" she proclaimed.

Dad had no choice but to turn his head back in my direction, but he bowed it at the same time, and I bowed mine, too. "See what?" he said.

"Would anyone like apple pie?" Mom asked, pointing desperately at the pie.

"Look up, dummy," Ann said, trying to nudge me with her voice.

Mom ignored Ann's taunt. "I'll warm the pie up in the oven and get the ice cream out of the freezer," she said.

"Don't go to all the trouble," Dad said. "Just let me have a small piece." He cleared all his food, including the untouched steak, off to one side of his plate to make room for dessert.

"Kids," Mom said, asking us to follow suit.

"Okay," we said in unison.

"Do you want it warmed over with ice cream?" Mom asked, relieved.

"Just like Dad's," we replied, also making room on our plates.

As Mom dished out the apple pie, we sat motionless, staring straight ahead. Once she finished, the three of us began eating the pie in silence, while Mom nibbled absentmindedly from the pie left in the pan. After devouring four bites, I raised my head to steal a few glances at Dad. My first peek was almost furtive, but I became bolder with each subsequent glance until my eyes were fixed on Dad.

My fork froze in mid-air.

What I saw was unmistakable.

Unmistakable—and devastating.

Something broke inside me.

My first cough was barely audible. But the second was louder, and the third and fourth came faster and faster until

The Announcers

my whole body was seized in a paroxysm. Almost convulsing, I knocked over the glass of milk a second time as I fled from the kitchen—and from my father—

I could hear Mom rushing to catch me—and Ann trailing behind—

But Dad…

Dad was left alone at the dinner table. I ran out, not sure what I was running from, not sure where I was running to. I just knew I couldn't breathe in that room and had to get out of there.

And everyone ran with me.

Except Dad. He was left behind, alone.

Even though I ran from him, trying to escape—I know now that, in a way, I never did. An important part of me never left that room.

Chapter 16

The memories are gradually fading away, and I find myself in the present. It's colder than before. Gray covers everything like a fog. I'd turn and walk back to the car if I could, but somehow that's not an option. It's so barren and desolate here—far more desolate than when I first started walking—like the surface of the moon. It feels airless, like I might stop breathing at any moment.

I tell myself that things will be better when I reach the ballpark. They have to be, because there's so much there waiting for me. Memory brings to mind all of Northside's details—the fence encircling the field, topped with freshly painted white wood; the mound of dirt in the right field corner; the concession booth where my parents bought treats for us after every game; the stands where Mom and Ann sat; and the scorekeeper's box itself, directly above and behind the backstop. Dad was always there.

My thoughts are floating back to that time—the start of my second year with the Nationals. I got new cleats because my feet had grown too big for the old ones. Mom washed my new uniform before I'd even worn it once.

Dad told me more than once of the pride he'd feel every time I stepped into the batter's box. He told me it was "far better than anything the doctor could order."

I failed to appreciate the irony of this, but then there was a lot Mom and Dad said and did that took me years to understand. Even if I took out the microscope Mom and Dad brought back for me from Minnesota and looked hard enough at the events of its time, it would still leave some things indistinct, out of focus. And I'm so conflicted about what they were trying to do for me and Ann... by not telling us... about Dad's condition... that no microscope will ever bring resolution.

I can't imagine what they went through, whether they argued or agreed, but I can picture the central question: "What do we tell Ann and Jack? Do we tell them?"

Yes... or no...

Ann and I were both so young, and Dad was dying. If they told us, how could we possibly understand? Would it have robbed us of something? This was a choice they were forced to make under the most difficult of circumstances. And they chose *No*.

They didn't tell us. One day led to another, one supper to the next catastrophe, followed by silent fury and tears, unexplained events piling up until there was no way to make it better—for Dad, for Mom, for Ann, for myself. I wish I could go back in time and fix things, make them better in any possible way, any way at all. That opportunity either never existed or was lost long ago, but the thought, the *need* to make things better won't leave my mind. And I'm aware that this need to somehow impossibly fix the past is grounded in the absurd feeling that what happened was, in some way, my fault.

If only I'd kept a journal back then, I could've written down everything that happened—particularly that first game I played in the second season—the best game I'd ever play. A journal might've made for good reading through all the years—and maybe then the good things wouldn't feel so fleeting.

The Announcers

That game against the Rangers was one of the best days of my life—and then it was gone.

Dad was gone, too.

Now everybody is gone, except Ann and me.

Vanished. Disappeared along with everything else that might provide memories for me. My baseball shoes and uniform, Ann's doll she got when I got my glove, so much more—every item packed up and stored away for no other reason than to collect dust.

A journal might spare me from straining to remember some details. Memories like polishing my cleats and oiling my glove. Looking at myself in the mirror after I'd put on my uniform. Making sure my bat, a black Louisville Slugger, was ready before each game. Laughing and joking with Mom in my room. Going outside and making sure there were no rain clouds on the horizon.

And somewhere close, hiding in the shadows, is the memory of Dad I'm seeking—the best one of them all.

In the world of *now*, I'm still that strange man shuffling down a cold Kokomo street. I'm three steps closer to the ballpark. I'm getting there, slowly but surely. It's only half a block before I make the left turn onto Tate Street. Riding with Dad, that left turn was the sure sign we were almost there. The park would be just ahead, waiting for me the same as always—

Whenever Dad and I reached this spot, my thoughts shifted to the upcoming game, and on the days when I wouldn't be up in the booth with Dad, it was almost as if he wasn't next to me—mentally, I was already out on the field, anticipating my turns at bat, how I'd play my position, and so on. I don't recall ever looking over at Dad and smiling at him or saying goodbye before jumping out of the Ford. If only one of those magic moments that other boys have with their dads had happened. They'd be so important to me now, across all these decades.

But instead I said nothing—*nothing*—because I naïvely assumed Dad would always be above me, announcing the game from the scorekeeper's booth while I played, and that he'd always return home with me afterward. It was almost a year after he'd died that I struggled with the question of where Dad might have gone, and here, again, nothing was a part of my thinking. *Where did Dad go?* After a long time, the answer came: *To nothingness.*

Nothingness has preyed heavily on my mind ever since—and emptiness is its echo.

This emptiness... It's the same way I felt when I discovered why Jimmy Campbell didn't return for the second season. Jimmy was the most gifted athlete on the team. After the first season was over, Dad said Jimmy wouldn't be coming back. I don't know why Dad knew this, but that doesn't matter. What does matter is what happened when I tried to find out why.

The first couple times I asked Dad why, he'd just say, "I'm not sure," then ramble on for a while as a sad, unchanging expression drifted across his face. Each time I asked, I thought I'd be told the reason, but after seven or eight attempts, I knew I'd come up against a stone wall and gave up. It was pure chance that I eventually found the answer.

Jimmy was the only black kid on my team. He was really beautiful, and it was a joy to watch him move and run, especially since I was such a slow runner. I'm sure now that he'd struggled in some way to make the team, but it seemed like he belonged there, and it was a mystery to me when he didn't

The Announcers

return.

One afternoon, I ran into a teammate downtown. I asked why Jimmy didn't come back to play. My teammate glared at me like I was a huge fool, then sighed deeply and pursed his lips: "He died."

I was stunned. Jimmy Campbell—dead. My teammate studied my face to determine my reaction, and seeing whatever he saw, quickly walked away from me. I looked at the ground, gathered my thoughts, then looked up and tried to call my teammate back, but it was too late—he'd disappeared down the street.

I looked back at the sidewalk, my thoughts repeating over and over, quietly.

Jimmy Campbell had died.

I mulled these words over in my mind, unable to comprehend—

He's dead— He's gone—

What had started out in my head as a simple matter of Jimmy not rejoining the Nationals suddenly exploded into something else entirely. My mind raced, grasping at disintegrating straws. *Not coming back? Not for the second season at all? Not even in the middle or maybe at the end? But why him? Why Jimmy? He hit a homer in his last game. He was doing so well! But why? WHY?*

"This... can't... be," I said haltingly. "No..."

But it was true, it was the way things were—and still are—and a single, deafening, relentless utterance filled my head:

YES.

Later on I learned Jimmy had died of leukemia—another

reality I didn't fully understand then. But even without understanding that disease, I knew what it did, knew its outcome, and realized that something was wrong—*something was terribly wrong*—and no one could explain why this was allowed to be. And even when I did muster up enough courage to voice my thoughts, the few people I asked either had no answer or told me to trust in God and His wisdom—

But how could I do that? How could I trust a god that was responsible for something so horrible as a child's death? And how could this entity, this something, this killer of children... how could this god be wise?

But I don't want to think about Jimmy now. I'm so close to the ballpark. I want something else on my mind when I first lay eyes on it. I need to call on a better memory to keep moving. I need to reach out for something that still feels new—a memory so strong, so real, I can almost touch it...

One's coming to me now—it's what I thought about earlier, the best game I played—the one that's stayed fresh in my mind for so many years: the big showdown with the Rangers.

I remember my sister calling me a worrywart that morning because even though the sky was all blue, I was afraid it was going to rain.

"Not a cloud in sight," she said, laughing at me. She kept laughing until I wanted to hit her, but I didn't. *Why bother,* I thought, and told her not to bug me because I had to get ready for my game. But Ann continued pestering me, poking my sides and tossing my gear around, until Mom stepped in at last.

"Kids! That's enough," she said, agitated. Ann stuck her

tongue out at me, but Mom didn't see that. She never saw anything Ann did.

Recalling this memory shouldn't hurt as much as it does. I've got less than a hundred yards to go, and then I'll be make the last turn—and, once I see the ballpark, all the pain will be a thing of the past… But *why* do I think that?

Ann finally settled down when Mom got out my uniform from the previous season. She immediately noticed a few grass stains on the knee that the washer hadn't removed. It was a little late for that then—and I can't say I wanted her to get rid of them either—but Mom seemed to read my mind.

"These are last year's stains," she said, "and make up a part of our past. You earned them, and I would *never* think of removing them." Though her voice was strong, I didn't realize that my mother was doing everything she could not to cry. She returned the uniform to its box. "This part of the past shouldn't be disturbed," she said, eyes glistening.

This careful preservation of my old uniform was typical of Mom, who definitely had her quirks, among them the compulsion to hold onto tangible reminders from time past.

Report cards, pictures, newspaper clippings, high school graduation caps, yearbooks, Ann's clothes, Hopalong Cassidy drinking glasses, children's records, *The Little Engine That Could,* childhood drawings and scribblings—to anyone else, this collection would've been a museum of the unwanted, but they mattered a great deal to Mom.

I wish I understood why. But I never really knew my mother, her family, or the story of her life. These were all conversations that never happened.

J. G. Perkins

In truth, for any real communication between us to have happened, we both would've had to learn another language. In 1950s Kokomo, the language we spoke just didn't seem to have the words... and we never did find them.

The Announcers

Chapter 17

"TAKE ME OUT TO THE BALL GAME
TAKE ME OUT TO THE CROWD."

The loudspeaker's kicked on again. I can hear Dad playing "Take Me Out to the Ball Game" over the loudspeaker like he did before the first game of my second season—my big game with the Rangers. I feel crazy hearing that same song... but since I *can*... Maybe if I believed in anything, or maybe if everything weren't so painful, I'd actually be able to call all of this... hallucination... the real thing. Maybe sanity is overrated.

I remember thinking I wanted to have an especially good game—maybe my very best—for Dad. It was important to me that I did. I told Mom about this sometime that morning, and she passed what I said along. I didn't learn about her and Dad's conversation until much, much later, but when I did, I found out that Dad had broken down and cried because of what I'd said.

I didn't know why it'd happened when it did, but the breakdown came when we were sitting in the living room of our house on Mulberry Street. The big game was over and Dad was in his smoking chair while I sat on the stool at his feet. His voice started out normal as he congratulated me for a great effort: two bases-loaded doubles and five RBIs. My best game ever, and I was proud of my performance. After Dad finished talking, I expected that to be it, but he was only warming up.

There was an uncomfortable pause, and I could tell Dad wanted to say something else but was having trouble. He had difficulty showing any emotion other than anger. He was trying to share feelings with me that he could barely even have. He could hardly talk and I was embarrassed at first, not knowing whether I should say something to him. I couldn't have said anything anyway, because I was having a hard time keeping control of my own emotions.

Tears suddenly started streaming down Dad's cheeks, but I pretended they weren't. His first two words resembled gasps: "You… have…" He then forced back a sob, inhaling deeply. I became increasingly uncomfortable as his voice became loud and clear that his words have remained at the front of my memory… even to this day—

"YOU'VE GIVEN ME THE GREATEST GIFT IMAGINABLE BY SIMPLY DOING WHAT YOU'VE DONE IN EVERY GAME YOU'VE PLAYED!"

They're still so clear, I'd swear he was next to me right now; I'd swear he just said them over the loudspeaker for the entire field—the entire town—to hear.

How I wish I could hear him say it again! And say it with more warmth—any sign of warmth would be appreciated now. The sky is so wretched. And I'm so cold—that certain kind of cold I've felt ever since Dad died.

Thinking back, there wasn't a cloud in the sky on the evening of the Ranger game. Not a single one. And the air was sticky—much more sticky than usual. So sticky, in fact, that my uniform made my skin itch even after I'd had it on for just a few minutes.

I didn't say anything about the itchiness as Dad and I rode to the park. I always rode in the front with Dad, including when Mom and Ann came to watch me play. But even when they were in the back seat, it felt like it was just Dad and me alone together. I loved riding to Northside with Dad; I loved everything about when we were at the park. For a couple of hours, we could forget everything except baseball. This was our private, isolated world, and this world possessed its own set of rules and rituals complete with their own mysterious symbols, the scorekeeper's marks. Dad taught me how to use these symbols so damn well, I'm mentally keeping score each and every time I watch a baseball game—keeping score and thinking of our time up in the booth together.

Nothing that plagued us at home plagued us at the park. It was our own private sanctuary. And it's just ten steps more until I make the turn. I need to collect my thoughts first. I'm cold and stiff, and each step is hard. But it's the weight of memories that's really slowing me down.

I remember what Dad said as we drove around this turn those forty years ago. "Good weather for a game," he said. "No sign of rain that I can see."

And like the kid I was, all I did was agree. "There isn't," I said. But there was so much more in that moment than just a cloud-free sky—so much more that I dismissed like it was nothing, so much more that's been lost to me until… now.

For no apparent reason, I glanced over at Dad. He'd slowed the Ford just enough to turn and stare directly at me with an intensity that bordered on frightening. And that was about all that registered with me—the intensity of the expression on his face—since I failed to notice the rest, failed to see or understand what was right in front of me—

J. G. Perkins

If I'd known then what I know now, I would've been able to see how incredibly important this moment was to him. I would've known what he'd felt but was unable to express to me in that moment: his enjoyment of all the moments we'd experienced together at Northside; his pride at seeing me mature as a person and player since the time I collided with the outfield fence; his hopes for the season ahead; and above all, his love— *his love!*— the love that he never could express openly to me for as long as he lived. But even if I couldn't understand his intensity, I could feel it in that moment, and it bore into me like a laser. And later, as a father myself, I would understand that intensity as love.

But there was something beyond love in that look. It was the sad gaze of knowing, of not being able to witness and participate in what was to come. He wouldn't be there to be my best man when I married my high school sweetheart. He wouldn't be there to watch me get my doctorate and find success in the world. He wouldn't be there to hold his grandson…

But all I could think to say at that time, with him staring at me, was that I hoped it stayed sunny for the game.

I remember what Dad said next, but I'm standing here, stupefied and frozen in the cold, waiting for him to answer me, waiting to hear his answer come flying over the loudspeaker. He's supposed to look at me and say, "It's a good bet it won't rain for the next several hours. No sure thing for anything after that." I want him to say it exactly as he did then, with the very same enunciation, the very same intonation—I can feel my mouth moving, articulating the words of these thoughts as I think them. What's happening to me? I feel like a puppet with no one working the strings.

The Announcers

The loudspeaker is silent, even though I'm straining as hard as I can to hear. There's nothing but quiet.

Nothing.

Always the nothing—surrounding me, enveloping me with a consistency as constant as death itself...

The last few times I visited Dad at the hospital, his door was shut when we got there. When we went inside, his stomach was so swollen, he looked as if he was going to have a baby. He was so much sicker than the last few times I'd seen him, sicker than anyone I'd see sick, sick and not being able to move without moaning. I remember this almost more than anything: Dad not being able to move in his hospital bed without moaning, moaning even when he wasn't moving. I remember he looked yellow, more yellow than before. After we left, I was scared and I didn't want to think about what I was thinking. Dad wouldn't be coming home for a long time. Dad... wouldn't... be coming home.

What was it he said next? What did he say right as we parked?

I saw a couple of teammates walking ahead. I felt compelled to join them and opened the door without giving Dad a second thought. After I set my cleats delicately on the concrete, Dad said, "Start the season off with a bang, son! Don't forget you're playing the Rangers!"

Dad's voice is so clear, I can't tell if that came from the loudspeaker or from my memories. But it doesn't matter—I feel like a ship freed from a sea of ice. Less than five steps before I make the turn. These are proving to be the most difficult so far, but maybe, maybe if I can hear Dad's voice again like that, I can finish those five steps like they're nothing.

Once I caught up with my teammates, I completely forgot about my family for a while. Eventually, when I was playing catch along the sidelines, I glanced up into the third-base stands and saw Mom and Ann. Ann was nibbling away on a lime popsicle—it's so green in my memory, it's practically neon—and it was dripping all over her, but she didn't seem to mind. I hoped Mom would give her a good chewing out for being such a slob, but if she did, I wasn't there to see it.

The next thing I knew, the coach was walking up to the mound with a bag of baseballs. "Batting practice!" he hollered. As he dropped the balls on the ground, I remember thinking about Dad taking out that Elvis record and playing "Hound Dog."

Whether I'm hallucinating or not, it'd be awfully nice to hear that song now.

But Dad must have read my mind back then, because before I could count to five, Elvis was blaring out over the loudspeaker. Mom said later that Dad had it turned up so loud she couldn't hear herself think, but Ann was yelling, "It's too loud!" at the top of her lungs, so at least you could hear *her* over the noise.

I half-expected Jimmy Campbell, my teammate who'd died of leukemia, to somehow sneak into the batter's box before I did. How stupid could I have been? But this didn't stop my imagination, and suddenly I saw him up there, taking his cuts. Each swing brought a *crack!* as his bat made contact with the ball. If only I could've left it at that. But I couldn't, and as soon as my imagination ran out of steam, Jimmy's image evaporated into thin air, right on the spot. And just before I stepped into the batter's box, I realized I would never see Jimmy again, and that thought—*I'll never see him again*—made it suddenly hard to breathe.

Spooked, I looked up at the scorekeeper's box to reassure myself that Dad was still there. I don't know why, but for an instant I wondered if he was gone, which was especially strange because Dad was always up there in the box. The sun made it almost impossible for me to see, and no matter how much I squinted, all I could make out was an outline of a shadow.

I couldn't see Dad, so for a second, I tried to imagine what it would be like if he wasn't there, if he was absent altogether. But I couldn't imagine it and gave up trying.

Little did I know at the time, but those thoughts were the first few in what would become a lifelong obsession of mine, an obsession that even infiltrated my dreams: an obsession with absence.

Mom is going to the hospital by herself... I ask her why Ann and I can't go, but she doesn't really answer me. When she gets home, I can tell she's been crying, but I don't say anything. Instead I ask her how Dad is, but all she does is turn her head away from me before saying... something. She had to be saying something because I heard words... but I don't want to listen. I'm crawling into my bed and under my blankets to feel safer, but it's not working. I'm unsafe... through the night... into the next morning... when Mom calls me into the living room...

My father was dying and would soon be dead.

After years of working in medicine, I should be familiar with death. I know all its ins and outs, and I might even qualify as an expert witness, like I have on other subjects. I should be familiar, but I'm still an amateur, I'm still a beginner, an absolute novice who's unable after all this time to adequately express how utterly devastating losing a father *was*. Was and *is*—

My bat felt different in my hands that evening. It was much lighter and perfectly balanced, and it'd be virtually impossible *not* to make contact with the ball. That bat was my good luck charm. I kept it in my closet and wouldn't take it out until game time. Everything seemed enchanted that night. Even the ball seemed larger than normal, like it was a softball. I loved to hit and couldn't wait for my first time at bat. Maybe my swing wasn't as good as Ted Williams's, but it got the job done. By the time I left the batter's box, I'd definitely found my groove. I knew it was going to be a good night at the plate for me. I just knew it.

I was boiling when I finished batting practice—literally drenched in sweat. I looked up into the stands where Mom and Ann were sitting, and I saw they both had Cokes. Later on, Mom said she could've fried an egg anywhere there was a vacant seat. There are few things hotter than the Indiana sun in summer.

And right now, as I try to move down the street, I feel as sluggish, as though that Indiana summer sun's been beating down on me for days. Even with all that heat back then, I didn't feel like my feet were made out of lead—I felt like my whole body was electric. As we lined up on the first-base line and Dad played "The Star-Spangled Banner," my toes kept tapping nervously and I fidgeted with my hat. I could barely stand still.

I hope that first-base line is still there exactly as it was, with its perfectly straight lines of chalk. I always felt bad about running on them. As I think about waiting on that base line now, so eager for the song to be over, I can almost hear it playing now, surging like my heart's trying pound right out of my chest—

"OH SAY CAN YOU SEE...

STARTING FOR THE NATIONALS

IN RIGHT FIELD, BATTING SIXTH,

NUMBER TWELVE."

That sounded like Dad—or was it me, mouthing my thoughts out loud? But the way things originally happened, he would've finished playing the anthem and *then* announced my turn at bat.

I don't want this to get confused. Not this memory. Not now. It's far too important for it to stay the way I remember it—opening day of our last Little League season together.

I asked Mom if I could go with her on that last day that Dad was in the hospital, but she still told me no. I could see there was no use arguing, so I didn't. She asked me if I wanted to go to the movies instead. What else could I do? Even though I didn't want to, I said yes. She was trying not to cry when I left. She was trying not to cry, but—

Before the game even started, I had a hunch that I was going to have a good game, but... I've said this before. It's so, so, so important that none of this get confused, but I've said this before...

mother is definitely crying   and shooing me out of the house before i can take a stand   and tell her i   don't want to go to

J. G. Perkins

the movies   and it's hot   as soon as i get outside   just as hot as the big day   i got two bases-loaded doubles   and five runs batted in   with dad sitting in the scorekeeper's booth above me   the way to the movies is the same way i go to school except this is summer   august twenty-first   thursday   the summer after my big game   mom's even arranged for the neighbor to go with me   mikey's his name   and so we walk like we're going to school until we get to where we'd turn except mikey and i are about to go straight   ahead   to downtown and the isis theatre   for a monster movie   two "ises"   dad always calls it   trying to make a big joke   a big joke i've never laughed at   never

but i want to now   more than anything in the world but it's too late   he's

in the hospital   and i   don't know   when i'll see him again...

I'm about to turn to the left to go to the ballpark. A half step is all that's left—all I do is complete that step, and then I turn. The ballpark will be straight ahead on the left... the ballpark where everything was—I'll look up at the backstop first, where Dad was for the games. Then I'll take in the outfield fence where I hit my head in tryouts. Then I'll look for the stands where Mom and Ann cheered for me during the game...

there's a   mulberry bush off to the side   of the corner where mikey and i   turn   to go to school   i always thought this was funny   since we live on mulberry street   but walnut is the street   we're walking on   a walnut tree should have been where the mulberry bush is   i say to mikey   but he's staring at me   like i'm nuts   but   but   and this is   important   a gust of wind   blows through the mulberry bush   it takes me   by surprise   no   much more than that

The Announcers

it's scaring me   something   s-something bad is happening incredibly incredibly bad   something i don't want to face something i   don't understand   oh god...

    Dad's about to announce me over the loudspeaker—I can feel it in my bones. I think I can hear Mom and Ann cheering in the stands. I've stopped. I'm at the corner. I'm turning, just as the car turned with Dad behind the wheel with me riding next to him so many years ago... It's going to be the same as it was then... It's going to be exactly the same, and the memory of him that I want, the one I can cherish, is going to come to life.

Chapter 18

The park is just up ahead. All I need to do now is complete my turn, walk a hundred or so feet, and I'll be there. Perhaps it'll be warmer up ahead. I certainly hope so. If it gets any colder, I'll break into pieces.

As I near the park, a moment's coming to me—one of the most important of my entire youth, maybe even my entire life. Odd how I can think that. I've had a family, a successful career, and real accomplishments, but here I am looking back to Little League as a high point. This was about to be my first at-bat with bases loaded. I'd been in the dugout, just waiting for something like this to happen. You don't get many chances like this. It might've been my imagination, but with the way the crowd was cheering, it seemed to me that they were expecting a big inning. Mom and Ann were among the loudest. Dad might have turned off the loudspeaker and joined in, but I never asked him if he did.

At the top of the third inning, the score was tied at 2–2. Someone had to get on base or else I'd have to wait until the next inning to bat. The seconds ticked off like they were trudging through molasses. The first batter up, Bobby Grant, walked on four straight pitches. None of them were close to the plate.

I can hear the umpire's voice yelling "Ball four!" across the decades. I can still see his chest protector barely concealing his double chin, too. After Bobby's walk, unless there was a double play, I'd get to bat. Bobby trotted to first base as I put on my batting helmet and walked out of the dugout. As I stepped out, I looked up to where Dad was, but I couldn't see him. Then I looked over and saw Mom and Ann waving at me. I waved back.

Up next, Butch Franklin hit a single, putting runners on first and second. I held my black Louisville Slugger in both hands as I walked to the on-deck circle. *Now we're ready for action.* The cheering was even louder than I'd heard minutes earlier. There was one more batter—Timmy Fletcher—and then I'd be up. I gripped my bat tighter and tighter as I watched.

Timmy managed to work up a full count before he beat out an infield grounder. *E-6* was how I scored it. Did Dad score it the same? I never got around to asking. Even though it's such a minor incident, this too is another blown chance.

I feel like I should be hearing Dad announcing me now—here, in this moment, and in my memory too—but it's not coming. Why is remembering this—*all* of this—proving to be so goddamn difficult? I've skipped over so many important details. What were we doing before batting practice? Posing for pictures? I can't remember.

Dad never liked having his picture taken. On family vacations or otherwise. It's easy to tell why—he was so thin and sickly in the few photographs I have of him. At least they were taken in black-and-white so I can't see the yellow tint of his skin.

Though my feet feel as if they could go out from under me at any second, in my mind I'm striding up to the plate again. Even if I can't hear Dad announce me, I'll never forget the pride in his voice every time he called, "Next batter for the Nationals—Number Twelve, Jack Lewis!" over the loudspeaker. I remember, too, how he told me after the game that there was no one he'd rather see "waltzin' up to the plate with three runners on base."

As they say in baseball parlance, the table was all set to clear. I remember slowly walking up to the plate, readjusting my batting helmet, my trusty bat in hand. As I made my way to the plate, I could hear the cheers.

"Wait for a good pitch!" Mom yelled out at me.

"Get a hit!" Ann screamed.

And then the umpire hollered "BATTER UP!" and motioned the pitcher to deliver the pitch. I could hear chatter coming from both sides.

I took one last look up toward Dad, but I couldn't see him.

I knocked the dirt from my cleats with the bat, and then settled in at the plate with a southpaw's stance—not Mantle's stance, not Musial's stance, and not Williams' stance, but *my* stance.

The runners led off their respective bases, and then came the first pitch—"BALL!"

I know it was the umpire who made the call, but when I remember it now, it's Dad's voice I hear. That's not the way it happened the first time... or is it? Mom and Ann yelled out, "Way to go! What an eye!" I can hear them say this even though I'll swing at anything to get a hit—just like Yogi Berra, another one of my favorite players. They kept cheering as the next pitch came roaring in—"FOUL BALL!"

I took a hefty swing at that one, even though it was over my head, and the ball ricocheted off the screen just below the scorekeeper's booth. Did Dad duck to get out of the way?

But then came the next pitch, and with it, Dad's announcement—

"THERE'S A DRIVE GOING INTO THE GAP IN DEEP LEFT CENTER FIELD—IT'S GOING TO BE IN THERE FOR EXTRA BASES—ONE RUNNER WILL SCORE—THE BALL'S ROLLING TO THE FENCE—*TWO* RUNNERS ARE IN—WILL A THIRD MAKE IT?—HERE'S THE THROW COMING IN FROM THE OUTFIELD—RUNNER STOPS AT THIRD—BATTER STOPS AT SECOND—ALL RUNNERS ARE SAFE, AND IT'S A STANDUP DOUBLE FOR MY BOY! THE SCORE IS NATIONALS FOUR, RANGERS TWO."

Did Dad really say "my boy" along with all the rest? As soon as my bat hit the ball, the crowd was roaring with applause, drowning out the loudspeaker, so I'm not sure what Dad did or didn't say—but I remember how I felt after I heard his announcement. Yes, I still remember my exact thoughts:

I DID IT!

I DID IT FOR YOU, DAD!

Are you proud of me?

For an instant I thought it might be a grand slam, but it didn't have enough force to carry the ball over the fence.

After my double, the Rangers called a timeout and their manager talked to the pitcher as if what I just did was his fault. There was nothing else for me to do, so I kicked second base with my cleats, sending up dust and chalk. My adrenaline

The Announcers

started to wear off, and I noticed the heat again, closing in around me like a hurricane. Gnats flew around my head, so I took a swipe at them—

Why gnats are still a part of this memory is beyond me, but there they are. And then, just as inconsequential, I remember checking on Mom and Ann in the stands and still not being able to see Dad even though I was looking for him the hardest.

And speaking of looking: although I'm almost at the ballpark now, I'm having trouble seeing it. Twenty or so feet ahead should be the start of the left-field fence, but I can't see any of it from where I'm standing now. Maybe this strange gray sky is to blame—not quite fog, not quite clouds, but obscuring things just the same.

My memories are leapfrogging ahead now, straight on up to the sixth inning, when I was sitting in the dugout facing the exact same situation as before: the bases were loaded again and I was the next batter up. I couldn't believe it. *It's like I'm living in a dream.*

No sooner did I find myself in the hole again than I heard Mom yelling, "Do it again, slugger!" I could hear Ann's follow-up too—"Do it again! Do it again!" But when I turned to look at them, they were standing up and cheering as if I'd already hit another two-run double. I waved and ignored them. But even after I turned around, I could feel their eyes upon me.

Everything was set up for me just like before, and to top it off, they were playing me for a dead pull hitter like they'd totally forgotten what I did to them last time. And then—

J. G. Perkins

"C C C C..."

Something's coming in over the loudspeaker! But it's so static-y... is it Dad again?

"C COMING U UP TO THE P P PLATE
T THE NATIONAL'S R RIGHT
F FIELDER N NUMBER SIX ER NUM—"

What's happening? This *isn't* how it's supposed to be. T*his isn't*—

But— but—

But suddenly the grayness is clearing and I can finally see the field.

I'm stepping forward to where the left-field fence should be...

But it's not there.

It's nothing but barren ground... dirt without grass... covered in broken beer bottles and shards of glass. If the sun was out, maybe they'd sparkle. But glittering broken glass is no substitute for the sun, or the stars, or the cheers I should be hearing, the cheers I heard as I walked up to bat that second time...

The entire crowd was cheering. I couldn't hear anyone this time—not Mom, not Ann, and still not Dad. But the umpire's yell—"BATTER UP!"—still could've burst my eardrums. I stepped up to the plate, took off my batting helmet, and saluted my father—

NO!

I didn't do that. But maybe I did? But the Rangers definitely called another timeout just as soon as I got into my stance.

The Announcers

They had a conference on the mound, then brought in a new pitcher. I can't remember his name, but it took him forever to warm up, and even once he was on the mound, the Rangers were still playing me for a pull hitter. Their chatter was louder than it was the first time.

Then came the first pitch—high and outside—ball one. I stepped back from the plate and knocked the dirt from my cleats. I could feel Dad's eyes zeroing in on the back of my neck as I got back into my stance. More chatter. In came the second pitch, and I swung and hit a line drive down the right-field line. Everyone on base went running full tilt. The crowd cheered louder than I'd ever heard.

"FOUL BALL!" the umpire called. That was a close one—only a matter of inches, a couple feet at most. The crowd was disappointed. The umpire called a timeout, and all the runners went back to their bases.

Now the count stood at 1–1. One ball, one strike. Bases full of Nationals. Not much longer now.

"Come on and get a hit!" Ann's voice projected above all the others. I could feel Dad's eyes on the back of my neck like the sun focused through a magnifying glass. Would this… be the last time… he'd watch me? I can't remember. I stepped out of the batter's box and saluted him—

No! It didn't happen this way. It didn't, but it should have!

Dad died and I was powerless to do anything about it. One second my father was alive, and the next he was dead. I was goddamn powerless and then there was nothing I could do about it. *Nothing.*

If only I'd saluted Dad then—I never had the chance to tell him goodbye. He asked to see Ann and me before the end came, but we weren't able to go.

The runners led from their bases. The chatter picked up again.

"Sand's blowin' in your face batter! Nothin' but sand, sand, sand. New guy getting ready to sit down—"

"BALL TWO!" the umpire yelled, and then the Rangers' coach called another timeout. He walked to the pitcher's mound, and this time the entire infield joined him. I stepped out of the batter's box, watching the action on the mound. The runners held their positions.

"Get ready!" Mom and Ann yelled. I looked up and waved again.

"PLAY BALL!"

The Rangers' manager headed back to the dugout, and all the players took their positions. I took off my batting helmet to try and see Dad. I couldn't.

The infield should be coming into view any second now. Twilight is gathering—it's getting hard to see—but—I know there's something of him, waiting in the scorekeeper's box.

I know he's up there.

"BATTER UP!"

Not Musial, not Mantle, not Williams, but me—me at the ready for a second go!

Mom was standing. "Wait for a good pitch!"

Ann was standing. "Do what you did last time!"

Dad was up above me in the scorekeeper's booth. Dad was up above me...

"BALL!"

I could hear the Rangers' coach's voice coming at me from their dugout. "Work on 'im! You got 'im where you want 'im!"

There was a lot riding on the next pitch. But I've already explained as much, explained that something special—unbelievingly and extraordinarily special—was about to happen. I was about to clear the bases.

Twilight is darkening, and Dad's scorekeeper's booth is just up ahead. A few more steps and I'll be where he was—is—

"All right... what do you... want me... to do?"

I can hear his voice again—but it's so weak—so weak and faint even though I'm so much closer to the booth. Maybe it wasn't him—maybe it was the wind, playing tricks... This isn't how it's supposed to be working out. Not after all the effort I've expended to get here. To have traveled so far and faced so many memories again to finally arrive where I've wanted to be all along and have Dad asking me what I want him to do, when he should be saying what he already said on that very special day.

Everything revolves around what I'm about to do, what I should have done the very time I had the opportunity. But for it to happen the way I want, he has to be in the exact spot he was so many years ago: in the scorekeeper's booth, with me in the batter's box. It has to play out this way for me to openly state how much I loved—*love*—him so that he will *know*. I never had a chance to tell him. I was waiting for him to come home from the hospital to say it, but I was never able to—

It all revolves around this! Yes, it has to. After so long. Yes. I loved you, Dad. I love you! This has been such a long time in coming. Almost my entire life. I had so much growing to do before I could appreciate that he loved—*loves*—me as much as it's humanly possible for a father to love a son.

There was so much I didn't understand, growing up while he was dying—so much that should have been so easy for me to see.

GODDAMN IT!

All I can hear is the chatter, the chatter!

"One more strike to go, batter-batter, then it's back to the dugout… ha ha ha… easy out... swing swing swing ... nothin' but air... air air air... swing batter... SWING... HAHAHA—"

A chorus of hateful voices… kids' voices… and nothing more…

NO!

There's so much more to it than this—Dad's ecstatic announcing, my teammates clearing the bases because of my doubles, the treats afterward with Mom and Ann—but now I'm standing where the field should be, or where I think it was, and there's nothing but cold, silence, and gathering darkness. And I can't seem to relive this memory without the field. I've realized it thousands of times in my head, but now that I'm here, and the field's not… the field's *nothing*…

I *know* I'm in the right spot. Off to the right was where Mom and Ann sat in the stands cheering, and ten or fifteen feet past that should be the scorekeeper's booth… where Dad should be. That's how it should be, how it has to be! I'm certain of it! But—

The Announcers

They're gone, as if I'm stranded on another planet.

Dad, I want to see you perched in the scorekeeper's booth *exactly* as you were. Can you imagine me thinking this, after all these years, when I'm now almost a quarter century older than you were back then? You'd be a young man compared to me now. *You were a young man when you died!*

But now it's flat as a table top where you were, where the scorekeeper's booth was, like nothing was ever there. There's not the slightest clue of your presence—not even a discarded pack of your matches—and I'm looking as hard as I can. But you've been gone for nearly fifty years.

Why do I attach such importance to the impossible…

There's something off to the side, on the ground. A long cylindrical shape—it's a rusted pipe. It must be the same pipe that supported the backstop, the backstop that protected Dad from foul balls, like the ones I dinged off my bat before my doubles—

This is all that once was.

There's nothing except this rusty backstop pipe. Dad's eyes *had* to stare at it more than once when he was alive. The pipe's half-buried in the ground like it's been fighting for all it's worth to stave off its own death. For how long? But this isn't important. What is that off to the east, in a cemetery, Dad's remains are totally buried, where they've always been.

My mind is struggling, but I feel like I'm beginning to bridge this gap between concepts, between the half-buried pipe that Dad saw with his own eyes and Dad always being dead. My mind is not only bridging them… but reconciling them too… merging them into a meaningful whole so that I can somehow… come together myself.

If not that, then what else can I possibly be seeking here?

What is it that I—

His approval.

I'm still seeking Dad's approval—his ultimate approval after all these years. Even though he's been dead for so long. But it was here, as I stood on second base after my second double, that I felt such approval. Even though I couldn't see Dad, I could feel his approval floating down on me from the scorekeeper's booth like all the sun's rays were on me at once.

But I never expected that warmth to leave me so quickly. I didn't expect *him* to leave so quickly.

I'm now looking out to where the field is supposed to be, where I stood on second base twice, searching for my father in the scorekeeper's booth, where I collided with the outfield fence during tryouts, where a thousand images should be wafting out of this dying day—but they aren't. They can't.

All there is a great expanse of nothing—

The brutality of nothing—

The scattered debris, the papers, the broken crates, the trash randomly and recklessly strewn throughout the years to produce this—the crassest defilement of something I wanted to be so special.

Nothingness is all there is.

Chapter 19

I waited for Dad to come home that first week he was in the hospital. Waited, hoped, and fully expected that one of those days he would surprise us by being all packed up and ready to go when Mom, Ann, and I arrived at St. Joseph's to visit him, and then everything would return to normal. But it never happened. Not in that first week, and definitely not during the second, when my hope faded for good.

Instead, Dad kept getting sicker and sicker until the last day I saw him. His stomach was swollen up so much it looked like it would pop. Even worse was how much Dad hurt when he moved. I'll never be able to forget this—him not being able to hide how much pain he was in no matter how hard he tried.

I was scared when I left him. I was scared knowing I'd never see him again. I was scared knowing he'd never be coming home.

Waiting for Dad to come home was replaced with another type of waiting—the worst kind. A few more days passed as Mom went to see Dad by herself and afterwards, when I was on the way to the movies, and a gust of wind blew through the mulberry bush. I knew Dad was dead. I knew he'd died at that very instant.

Dad was dead.

Dad was dead.

Dad was dead.

Mom brought his stuff home from the hospital.

there were people talking   crying   things   constantly

J. G. Perkins

*swirling around me   people   and things   and crying
and no dad   swirling   ripping   tearing at me so much I
wanted them to leave me alone   but they   didn't
couldn't wouldn't*

And now, finally, there's this: having to leave for the funeral home to say goodbye to Dad.

say goodbye   that's a phrase someone used   i forget who

to say goodby   as if dad will be waving to us before he leaves

i don't want to go   but mom has laid out   all my clothes for me

pants   sports jacket   trousers   and shirt   all neatly arranged on my bed   it's there so i can't climb in and hide under the covers i've spent most of the day wheezing and gasping for breath   in the bathroom i've managed to stop   and now i'm   in the living room   uncle norman's   talking to me   i don't know   who else is here   or where mom is   he tells me   i need to be strong   for mom   i know in my heart that's true   i'll always be strong for her   he says mom is   my responsibility now   i know in my heart that's true i'll always be responsible for her

now i'm standing   in front of the hallway mirror   in my sunday best

dad will   would   be proud of me   maybe   just maybe   dad will walk in

the front door   with his pipe in hand   tell me to change back   into my regular clothes

there was a big misunderstanding   he'll say to me smiling   and i've straightened everything and everyone out

The Announcers

      everyone and   everything   including dad not being dead

    music to my ears   except   mom is coming to get me

    dad is nowhere to be found

    dad ?

    the summer heat   attacks us   as soon as we walk out the back door

    we drive down a steep hill   at the funeral home we're the first

    to arrive   the parking lot is empty   i've already sweated through my shirt   probably my pants too   the funeral home looks like   a great big house   there's a sign

    penn's funeral home   shrubs and shade trees   surround the porch   two gigantic limousines are parked   to the side

      mom   ann   and i walk in   the front door   it's so stuffy i can barely breathe   i can smell flowers   right away   i don't like it   we follow the signs for   tommy lewis

    can they mean dad   ?

    can   they mean   that

    mr penn   is coming out to greet us   his brother owns   my favorite drugstore   in town   i got a free malt   after my two bases-loaded doubles   mr penn isn't making any noise   as he walks towards us   i look down at his feet   and see the thick   cushy carpet   that's   soaking up the sound   it's dark green   i don't like this   i   don't want him to but   he's starting to talk

    to mom   in a deep voice   the   final   arrangements have been made mr penn looks mad   i don't like him he looks   like a vulture   but mom   mom is   thanking him   why what for

   dad where are you

   now we're going   into a big room   chairs are neatly spaced   against two long walls   how many people would they hold   i wonder   i'm   looking   up up to   the front   to where   there's   a bronze casket   with flowers   on three sides   this must be where   the flower

smell   is coming from   it would suit me   just fine to never smell flowers again

   i'm looking   closer   the casket is shiny   and has yellow   satin on one end   someone's decided   to keep open why

   wait

   wait   a   minute

   dad

   is   that   you   inside

   what are you   doing   in there

   i can   barely see the outline   of his head it's resting on a pillow   mom's suggesting that i   get closer   so i can see better   and so   i'm going   i'm   almost all   the way   to the front of the room   where   dad   is but   mom's   not with me   neither is   ann   i'm all by   myself

   dad

   dad   where   are   you

The Announcers

 i'm feeling strange and different walking toward you dad so so i'm praying to god and jesus i think they said sometime at church that this would help that it would help to pray sometime someone said it would help i can't remember who but it's not helping dad hasn't budged one inch not one he's as still as a stone but even so i'm still praying until i'm standing above him in his coffin

 dad dad

 you're not moving and dead

 mom said that they'll be putting you in the ground in three days three days before i won't be able to see you again ever

 before i stop seeing your head looking like it's glued to the satin pillow

 before i stop seeing your face that looks so handsome without the sickness so handsome you're wearing the same brown suit and tie you usually wore to church

 i hate the smell of these flowers it's quiet and i'm so alone more alone than i've ever felt no one's standing beside me in the silence there's nothing but silence nothing i'm standing above you and not crying

 not crying because i'm responsible now i'm the man of the house now that you're no longer with us

 this is what uncle norman said to me
 I can't cry

J. G. Perkins

 can't cry while i'm standing above you and holding all my emotions inside

 feeling

 feeling only pain

 grandpa lewis is motioning for me to come over i feel guilty for leaving dad behind but i walk over towards them grandpa is trying to tell me how sorry he is trying because i can tell how uncomfortable he is and sad then he and grandma walk up to the coffin to be where i was before to stand over dad

 i can see dad's still not moving even when they get there grandma and grandpa begin to cry their shoulders begin to shake they start to sob i look over

 at mom and she's crying too but i'm not

 i want to more than i ever have in my life

 grandma's wailing why him and not me? why him and not me? her voice is overpowering the room overpowering me i want to run and hide but i can't she can barely stand but she stops wailing i can hear its echo grandpa is leading her away from dad's casket

 i can't watch them anymore i can't watch

 much of anything anymore

 a crowd of people file into the room

 why is mr penn letting so many people come in here they're all stopping to sign a book mom whispers to me

 two more days of this to go before dad's burial and then the worst torture there could possibly be but we have

The Announcers

no other choice

the guests file in   *everyoneeverywhere*   *says things that don't sound right*   *don't feel true*   *a voice inside me starts to answer*

how i've grown	*but I haven't*
there's no pain where your dad is now	*dad isn't anywhere*
he's in a better place	*no he's not*
you'll see him again someday	*no i won't*
he's looking down on you now	*no he isn't*
god is good in his mercy	*what mercy?*

i can't listen to this

i try to tune it all out ignore it but but it's replaced by something worse the people who pass me by without saying anything they don't have any words left to use they smile weakly why do they smile what are they smiling about

the funeral

i wake up

a hole in the ground where they'll take him to be buried

i'll never be able to see him again—

i dress in silence in my scratchy suit this time trying not to listen but i can hear mom crying in the bathroom i go to see if she's alright she must hear me because she stops

J. G. Perkins

 i ask her anyway

 she comes out and tells me she's fine her eyes are swollen
i ask her if there is anything i can do she's shaking
her head no shaking her head real hard

 i can hear a car door thumping shut norman's
here to take us i was hoping he'd forget we could drive
ourselves if we had to mom has driven us each day
we went to the viewing

 i don't like to think of riding in norman's
pontiac i don't like to think of doing anything
different but now norman is taking us a
different way than we went before if i could get
out of the car and run i would run run and
keep on running

 it's morning but a lot of people are out on the
streets they're all staring at us they're all staring
at me they must know where we're going
 they must know that dad is dead and going to be
buried it's like they're talking to me talking directly to me
and saying isn't it a shame about tommy lewis he
suffered so much and will be buried today look at how
young those kids are without a father it's a blessing that
he's up in heaven with god

 i can't stop hearing all of them say this can't
stop

 norman's parking in front of the funeral home
instead of the lot across the street i don't like this but
it wouldn't do any good to say anything

 ours is the only car in front except for two large

The Announcers

*black   limos   there are   small   green and white   flags
that say   no parking   funeral today
     but we're here now   and   not moving
     dad   never moved   in his casket
     mom is telling me   the car parked   next to the entrance
is called   a hearse   i can figure out   on my own   what
it's for   it's backed up   so its double doors   are against
a loading platform   this is where the   what's the word
pallbearers   will put   the casket   into the back   of the
hearse   after   the service   is over
     dad   where are you   i want you here   beside me
more than anything
     i have to be strong   no matter   how i'm feeling
     i know i have to be strong for mom
     in this suit   i'm frying like i'm in an oven   we're inside
finally   mr penn   is motioning for us   to follow him
but not norman   mr penn looks   like a vulture   he
makes   me wish   norman   would   come with us
mr penn is   leading us   into a big room   it must be
his office   but   someone's already in here   sitting in a
chair   who is it   his face is   turning toward us   it's the
preacher from the church   reverend prescott   i   should have
known   he'd be here   mr penn's saying   he has to attend
to some   last-minute arrangements   he's leaving
     i don't like   the sound   of the closing door   it reminds me
of the lid   closing   on dad's   casket
     the preacher is   rising   from his chair   to greet us   he
points to   three chairs   in front   of him   and tells   us
to be seated   his voice is   much more serious   than i
ever heard it   in church   his face   he's starting*

J. G. Perkins

to pray

 dad can you hear him?   can you hear him   praying to god   who   in his infinite mercy   is being asked   to help us   through this   difficult time

 if god has   infinite mercy   why did   dad   die?

 now reverend prescott   is thanking god   for delivering one of his most faithful   and deserving sons   to the   place   where   there is neither   suffering nor pain   why didn't god stop   dad's pain   the last time   i saw him   in the hospital

 there's organ music   coming through   the door people must be   on the other side   more people   i want them   to go away go and stay away   forever

 the prayer is   over   but   reverend prescott is   talking he's   telling

 us   we could come   into the church   later on   and see him   if we   need to

 but this is

  the last thing

   i

     ever

       want

         to do

 i can hear   voices   coming through   the door   with the music   now   the people   are in   the other room   and haven't   gone away   they must be   waiting   for us

The Announcers

mom's telling the preacher that we're all doing well but how could she be saying this when it's not true the sounds from outside are mingling with the preacher's voice he's going over the verses from the bible that he'll soon read soon before dad will be carried out to the hearse in his casket and—

i'm trying to ignore reverend prescott and figure out who's talking in the other room suddenly the organ stops playing and the people stop talking

it's time for us to go

we're going through a passageway that leads to yet another door and suddenly we're inside the room and can't turn back

and

nothing else is the same as it was

everything inside the room is different the chairs are different the flowers are different and they've moved dad moved his casket closer to the door

i'm staring at the carpet as i walk to my reserved seat i sit down escape is impossible i won't can't am looking at the coffin sitting directly in front of me the coffin and its contents as they are and will be forever in the ground

dad ?

it is no more than fifteen feet away from me my eyes can't help but go to where

J. G. Perkins

i can't   bring myself   to say   or think it
no smile   eyes shut
    both   things   still   the same   as when   i saw them
two days ago   it seems   much longer much much longer
but isn't they haven't   changed   after all   the goodbyes
      after all   the crying   after   the first time
i saw
       the preacher   is standing   at the podium   to my right
he nods   and   the organ music   stops   he's   asking
everyone   to rise   i   can't   believe what   i'm
hearing   he's saying   the same prayer   to god   that
he said   for us   a couple   minutes ago   to the
same god   who's   forgotten   and needs   a reminder
     ?
      he says   amen   and stops   repeating   that   same
prayer   he's   looking   straight ahead   and wants
our   undivided   attention   even more   than when
he was praying   i wouldn't   give it to him   if i wasn't
sitting in   the front row   with everyone   able to   see
me
      they're   all   quiet
      they're   all   waiting
      me   too   i guess   waiting   until—
      i see   reverend prescott   grasp   the front   of
the podium   so hard   that his knuckles   turn white
      he's   so close   i can   almost   touch him
      we're all   waiting for   the longest   time   and
finally
      we are gathered together   reverend prescott is saying   his

The Announcers

voice like   claps of thunder   to say goodbye   to a friend
and loved one   he's speaking   slow   and deliberate   i
can see   sweat   running down   his brow   sweat   is
soaking   my shirt

    i see   a bronze casket   holding   a dead body
that used to be   my father

    i hear   promises   of hope   and salvation i see
the side   of a face   that   a little more   than   a year ago
watched me   hit two   bases-loaded   doubles
a face that   is frozen   in a mask   that can   only become
alive again   in my mind   and   nowhere   else
    like   make   believe

    reverend prescott's   talking   about dad   about   his
life   but   the reverend doesn't know much at all   about
dad   it doesn't   ring true   how can he not know   why
hasn't he   gone to the trouble   of knowing

    where is   god   i can't listen   to another word
can't hear   another word   i can't hear   anything at all

    i can see   the reverend's   lips moving   and if   i look
i can see   other people moving   whispering   but

    the world   has no sound

Chapter 20

My thumb is rubbing across the rusty surface of the old pipe—the thick, sturdy pipe that once supported the announcer's booth where my dad once sat. Gripped in my hand, the pipe is cold, comfortless. I didn't sense it initially, but I was using it to brace myself against the treacherous footing of the trash-strewn junkyard that used to be Northside ballpark, to brace myself against the weight of memories. How long have I been here? The stars give enough light to illuminate the desolation, but they give no hint about time.

My body is stiff from being out in the cold, and I've closed my eyes to shut out the stars. I'm as alone now as I was at the end of my dad's funeral. As alone now, under the quiet unseeing stars, as I was in the church, surrounded by hundreds of mourners, when I had to shut out the noise to hear the truth.

The pipe, my grip firm upon it, anchors me to the present.

When Dad died, I hadn't been ready to let go of the possibility that what I had been taught about everlasting life might be true. I fought to believe, praying to God for a sign—*any* sign that Dad still existed somewhere. If there was a trace of him anywhere, it would've been his pipe, still smelling of his tobacco, imbued with his very breath.

It was so simple. I set his pipe on my dresser, and I prayed night after night for it to move. All I wanted—*needed*—was one small shift in its position to hang on to faith. To sustain my last hope that the world I'd been raised to believe in wasn't a lie.

Night after night, it didn't move.

Not an inch.

Not a fraction of an inch.

Nothing.

A faint hint of wind brings me back to the field; my hand cramping, squeezed tight on the rusty pipe, brings focus back to the *now*. At first I'd thought that what brought me back to Kokomo was Uncle Mike's funeral. It's clear now that isn't the case. I didn't even come back here for Dad. Why am I here?

My breath draws sharp and hard as I realize that after all this time, part of me *never* let go. In so many ways I'm still holding on to Dad's pipe, and all the hope that I've instilled in it.

I remember that I've been here before, that I don't need false faith and empty support. The pipe's lip digs into my palm and I let go, pushing myself away to stand on my own.

I've done this before—

on this same field, on this same spot—

so many years before.

I see myself, years ago, on the neatly mown grass of the field with its perfect, straight, white lines. I see myself, small, furious, alone, heartbroken, standing right here on the field below the announcer's booth.

My young voice, needing no microphone, amplified by pain and anger, announced to the sky,

"YOU DON'T EXIST!"

It was only logical. How could a benevolent God exist if life is unfair? How could a benevolent God exist when life is limited and everyone suffers? How could a benevolent God exist if he wouldn't answer my prayers?

My young self didn't have answers. I had questions, powerful questions.

The Announcers

I remember that young boy who reacted in hurt and anger at the loss of his father and his childhood—that young boy who would, from that day forth, walk about Kokomo, God's country, saying there was no God. The boy who set himself apart from friends, employers, teachers, everyone. The boy who was not afraid to ask questions about the relationship between emptiness, eternity, and nothingness.

For many young people, a rejection of something so huge would cause them to reject everything linked to and built upon it, in this case: family, love, hard work, honesty.

Looking back, I have to give my young self credit. Even when he was heartbroken, he could tell the difference between truth and falsehood. Even though our family had experienced tragedy, he did not reject family. He did not reject hard work. He did not reject honesty. Above all else, he never rejected love. He held on to what felt true and real.

My younger self also knew that my dad's skin may have been yellow, but he wasn't a coward. I saw him stare down death without the comforting belief in an afterlife. If he could face death without illusions, I knew even then that I could do the same thing with life.

As a man, I may not be at peace—but now I see the truth. I know now why I'm here. I'm here for myself.

Even though the word sticks in my mouth, I am here to affirm faith. Another kind of faith.

Faith in myself.

The godless void isn't empty.

I am here.

Publisher's Afterword

The Announcers is more than a first novel. It is the inaugural volume in one of the largest bodies of fiction ever created by a single author—the 19-volume *Darkness Before Mourning* series. By the time editing of the approximately 10,000 pages of manuscripts is completed for publication, it is projected that the work will approximate the size of Marcel Proust's *In Search of Lost Time.*

Beyond sheer size, the *Darkness Before Mourning* series is unusual in a number of respects. Among these are the method and manner of its creation. J. Greg Perkins, a successful pharmaceutical executive, arose and began writing each morning at 4 a.m. For some forty years, he wrote book after book, covering events in his life between 1955 and 2010. Unlike most authors, he was not writing for the public, or even with a reader in mind. As he says:

"Writing and remembering are the only way I have to keep my lost loved ones alive. Perhaps that is why, forty years after starting this work, I have never been able to stop."

When he finished a book, he put it in the bottom of his closet, showed it to no one, and started the next. I first learned of this huge body of work several years ago, and immediately felt compelled to bring it to publication, without ever being quite sure which among these many reasons is the most important—its size; the unique process and purpose of its creation; the author's unusual life story; the years of American history it spans; the unmitigated starkness of the narrative; some unusual approaches to prose. The thought comes to mind every time I look at it.

Celebrated novelist Lindsay Hill asked perhaps the essential question:

"I can't remember ever encountering a more direct, anguished exposition of unresolvable loss. My heart broke many times as I read. Also, as I read, the purpose (if such a thing can be spoken of) of the writing came repeatedly into question: was the work concerned with its relationship to the reader or was it, as implied along the way, more principally (along with his writing regimen) serving as a tether to sanity for the author? Or was it both in some degree of balance?"

A work of this size would be a stretch for any publisher, and it offers particular challenges to a new, small house like Chatwin. Publication of this book would not have been possible without the efforts of the following—my co-founder at Chatwin, Annie Brulé; cover designer Stephanie Podmore; Gregg Andrews, who managed to digitize the more ancient typewritten manuscripts; Molly Hunt, for so many things; Nicole Sarrocco and Mary Camezon for their incisive critiques; the folks at Square Books in Oxford, Mississippi for hosting the kickoff; Sean Perkins for his counsel; and Dean Kelly who does everything so must have done something.

But most of all, it's important for me to thank my co-editor, Geoff Wallace, who spent a year bravely wading into the 10,000 unedited pages of this enormous work. And last, but certainly not least, all of us at Chatwin are so pleased to thank our friend and colleague Amanda Knox for her exemplary work on this project.

Phil Bevis
Publisher, Chatwin Books

CPSIA information can be obtained
at www.ICGtesting.com
Printed in the USA
FSOW01n0801200715
9001FS